BAD ENGAGEMENT

ELISE FABER

SNARKY BOOKS FOR SNARKY MINDS

BAD ENGAGEMENT
BY ELISE FABER
Newsletter sign-up

BAD ENGAGEMENT
Copyright © 2020 Elise Faber
Print ISBN-13: 978-1-946140-71-5
Ebook ISBN-13: 978-1-946140-72-2
Cover Art by Jena Brignola

BILLIONAIRE'S CLUB

Bad Night Stand

Bad Breakup

Bad Husband

Bad Hookup

Bad Divorce

Bad Fiancé

Bad Boyfriend

Bad Blind Date

Bad Wedding

Bad Engagement

Bad Bridesmaid

BILLIONAIRE'S CLUB CAST OF CHARACTERS

Heroes and Heroines:

Abigail Roberts (Bad Night Stand) — founding member of the Sextant, hates wine, loves crocheting

Jordan O'Keith (Bad Night Stand) — Heather's brother, former owner of RoboTech

Cecilia (CeCe) Thiele (Bad Breakup) — former nanny to Hunter, talented artist

Colin McGregor (Bad Breakup) — Scottish duke, owner of McGregor Enterprises

Heather O'Keith (Bad Husband) — CEO of RoboTech, Jordan's sister

Clay Steele (Bad Husband) — Heather's business rival, CEO of Steele Technologies

Kay (Bad Date) — romance writer, hates to be stood up

Garret Williams (Bad Date) — former rugby player

Rachel Morris (Bad Hookup) — Heather's assistant, super-powers include being ultra-organized

Sebastian (Bas) Scott (Bad Hookup) — Devon Scott's brother, Clay's assistant

Rebecca (Bec) Darden (Bad Divorce) — kickass lawyer, New York roots

Luke Pearson (Bad Divorce) — Southern gentleman, CEO Pearson Energies

Seraphina Delgado (Bad Fiancé) — romantic to the core, looks like a bombshell, but even prettier on the inside

Tate Connor (Bad Fiancé) — tech genius, scared to be burned by love

Lorelai (Bad Text) — drunk texts don't make her happy

Logan Smith (Bad Text) — former military, sometimes drunk texts are for the best

Kelsey Scott (Bad Boyfriend) — Bas and Devon's sister, engineer at RoboTech, brilliant

Tanner Pearson (Bad Boyfriend) — Bas and Devon's childhood friend, photographer

Trix Donovan (Bad Blind Date) — Heather's sister, Jordan's half-sister, nurse who worked in war zones, poverty-stricken areas, and abroad for almost a decade

Jet Hansen (Bad Blind Date) — a doctor Trix worked with

Molly Miller (Bad Wedding) — owner of Molly's, a kickass bakery in San Francisco

Jackson Davis (Bad Wedding) — Molly's ex-fiancé

Kate McLeod (Bad Engagement) — Kelsey's college friend, advertiser extraordinaire, loves purple and Hermione Granger

Jaime Huntingon (Bad Engagement) — vet, does excellent man-bun

Additional Characters:

George O'Keith — Jordan's dad

Hunter O'Keith — Jordan's nephew
Bridget McGregor — Colin's mom
Lena McGregor — Colin's sister
Bobby Donovan — Heather's half and Trix's full brother
Frances and Sugar Delgado — Sera's parents
Devon Scott — Kels and Bas's brother
Becca Scott — Kels and Bas's sister in law
Heidi Greene — Kels' friend since college
Cora Hutchins — Kels' friend since childhood

ONE

Kate

DISGUSTED, she walked out of the bakery.

Mostly with herself for being jealous of the clearly happy couple.

Although, partly because they were so *ridiculously* happy. Come *on*. Who looked into each other's eyes with such devotion and joy while getting married in a freaking bakery with mostly strangers looking on?

No white dress or cake—counterintuitive as that sounded, considering they were getting married in a freaking bakery.

No flowers, which would be Kate's weakness because she loved gardening and arranging flowers, having spent most of her extra money on sprucing up her back yard.

The inside might be a bit of a disaster.

But the back yard was a lush, gorgeous retreat.

Not that it mattered because she didn't have anyone to share it with. Least of all, a gorgeous hunk of a man who stared at her with love in his eyes and tenderness in his smile.

Yes, she was bitter.

So, it was the perfect time for her cell to ring, her mother on the line.

Deal with the torture now? Or wait until it frothed to full power later?

She was already cranky and jaded and in a bad mood, so she might as well deal with her loving, but very nosy and interfering mother now. No sense in wasting a good mood later.

Because there *would* be a later.

Her mother loved her, that was never in doubt. What could *possibly* be questioned was the amount of attention she gave to her grown children's lives.

Attention that was now squarely focused on Kate.

On the fact that she was single when her two younger siblings were happily married, and her younger sister had recently popped out a kid.

Impressive. Beautiful—which she knew because she'd been in the delivery room.

But also . . . not *her*.

Hence, the increase in motherly calling.

Sighing, Kate swiped a finger across the screen and put her phone to her ear. "Hey, Mom."

"I've got the perfect man for you to bring to the Christmas party. He's a doctor and . . ."

Her mother continued talking, expounding on all of the wonderfulness that was this doctor. The trouble was that Kate was done with being set up. Her family was great at finding their own soul mates, their own happily ever afters . . . unfortunately, that same ability didn't extend to her.

Either *by* her or *for* her.

It never failed to end in disaster. Both for her *and* for her date.

So, as much as she longed to have a man she could call her own, one who'd call her his in return . . . she was taking a break from dating, from men, and most definitely from being set up.

"Mom," she began. "I'm not actually—"

"He's a doctor, isn't bald, and can have a conversation about something other than himself, Katie," her mother said. "He is a catch."

Who would turn into the world's worst asshole when he was around her.

Because that was her superpower.

Transforming seemingly *wonderful* men into lying, cheating, arrogant, self-centered, mansplaining, assholes.

And being that lightning didn't tend to strike the same place multiple times, Kate had decided on a hiatus from the opposite sex. Some time to sort out what was happening inside of her to make everyone she dated turn into a jerk.

This wasn't about all men on the planet being the bad guys, or her always picking wrong, or even about her family trying to set her up with a bunch of douche canoes. There was something wrong inside of *her*, something intrinsically wrong with the way she interacted with the men in her life.

So, a break.

Time to figure her shit out.

It was just . . . Christmas.

All of her family in one place. The huge party with the whole neighborhood. Everyone paired off and happy and gathering under the mistletoe her mother hung in each and every doorway.

And her.

Alone.

The pitying gazes plentiful.

Or worse . . . the copious conversations where all the happy people constantly threw every single male with half a brain cell in Kate's direction.

My cousin is in town and fresh out of a relationship . . .

I have a coworker who's new to the area. He's looking for someone . . .

My ex-husband would be perfect for you—no really, he's actually a great guy . . .

And more.

Kate just couldn't take it, couldn't stand the idea of another Christmas party at her parents' house matched with someone who didn't fit her, or worse, spending the entire extravaganza alone and in the corner, playing wallflower.

She wanted excitement.

She wanted someone who could be unequivocally hers.

She wanted someone who saw inside her and didn't run off in a panic.

". . . and Katie, love, he's going to be at dinner this Friday so that you two can get to know each other better—"

Fucking hell.

Family dinner *and* the Christmas Extravaganza?

Please. God. *No.*

"Um, Mom—"

"Remember he's got all his hair—"

"Actually, Mom. I'm kind of seeing—"

"And his stomach doesn't hang over his belt—"

"That's not—I don't really care about that—"

"*And* he's got the loveliest blue—"

"I'm engaged!" she screamed, cutting off her mother's soliloquy of all things doctor, and successfully drawing the attention of random strangers on the sidewalk. Which was a hard thing to do in San Francisco—because it was San Francisco, and these streets had seen a lot of shit—but also could only further confirm that she'd screamed it like a complete and total lunatic.

Shrieking *I'm engaged* on street corners.

What every man wanted.

It was a wonder she was single.

"Katie?" her mom asked. "Did you say you're engaged?"

No. No, she wasn't. Not even close. She was on a break from anyone with a Y chromosome, mostly to save them from herself.

But also . . . there was joy in her mom's tone.

Absolute joy that she had never heard directed at her. She'd heard it leveled toward her siblings. To her brother, when he'd announced he was proposing to Steph, who was really fucking cool and way too good for her brother—something he'd be the first to admit . . . because he was really fucking cool. She'd heard it expounded lavishly again at his wedding this last summer (during which Kate had spent her time fending off the worst setup of all setups, The Can't Take No For An Answer Setup). And obviously, it had rung with crystal clarity in her ears when her sister had announced she was pregnant, and again after her adorable niece had been born.

But her mom had *never* given it to Kate.

Which was probably the reason she let the crazy keep rolling along instead of stopping the joy in its tracks with the truth.

Why instead of saying, "No, Mom. You heard wrong," she said, "Yes, I am, and you'll get to meet him Friday at dinner."

Horror flowed through her as intensely as her mother's excitement poured through the airwaves, expressing her *joy* at meeting him, her *joy* at Kate having finally found a slice of her own happy.

"What's his name, honey?"

Oh fuck.

"What's that?" Kate asked, panic swarming to overtake horror. "You're breaking up."

Oh shit. *Oh shit.* She hadn't thought this through. She needed—

"I asked his name—"

"Hello?" More panic. More horror. More pretending the call was cutting out because she had to end this conversation now. Hell, she should have never picked up the call in the first place. "Mom? *Hello?*"

"Katie!"

Shit. Shit. *Shit.* "I can't hear you," she said. "If you can hear me, I'll call you later." She hung up.

Call her later.

Ha.

More like never.

As in, she'd *never* call her family again. As in, she was moving to a deserted island and changing her name and living off the grid in a tent with the most technically advanced thing being one of those compostable toilets.

Fuck.

She hated camping.

Which meant . . . she'd be there at the family dinner.

Because despite all of the setups and the pity and the fact that they'd found their happy, she loved her family. So. Damned. Much. And she also loved that stupid fucking Christmas party, even when she was lonely.

"*Ugh.*" Kate groaned, feet sliding to a stop on that dirty San Franciscan sidewalk.

She had a choice here.

She also knew she wasn't going to make the right one.

Because, instead of calling her mother back and telling her that she wasn't engaged, Kate opened Instagram, tapped on the profile of a man she'd been following for a while now, who'd followed her back and commented on a few of her posts, and . . . sent a message.

Later, she'd want to pretend she'd been drinking.

But in *that* moment, the only thing she was consumed with was desperation.

And lust. She couldn't deny lust was also her downfall.

Because surprisingly, shockingly, *insanely* the man from social media, the one whose abs had made her fall just a little in love with him, who had an actual man bun, but not one of those gross, greasy ones that looked like octopus tentacles—a nice one, sleek and shiny and way better than any bun she could wrestle her own locks into. But anyway, that handsome stranger . . .

He said yes.

And suddenly, Kate had a fiancé.

TWO

Kate

"WHAT AM I DOING?" she asked herself two days later. "Oh my God, what am I doing?"

She was going on her first date . . . with her fiancé.

Incongruous.

She couldn't believe that *JaimetheVet*—his Insta handle—and Jaime, her fake fiancé, and Jaime, the man whose last name she didn't know, had agreed to the plan. Moreover, she couldn't believe she was going.

He might be a serial killer.

He might drug her drink, bring her home, and tie her up in his basement.

Except, homes in California didn't usually have basements, so that was probably unlikely. And pretty though he may be, she couldn't imagine that Jaime the Vet was lying in wait for potential victims to DM him and ask him to agree to an elaborate ruse as someone's fiancé.

Which brought her back to . . . why had he agreed to do this in the first place?

Her phone chimed with the alarm she'd set for herself, the one whose label said, "Will You Stay Or Will You Go?" and Kate knew she had to stop thinking herself into knots and start making decisions.

Was she going through with the insanity?

No, she couldn't.

Except . . . she didn't want to stand him up. Jaime the Vet seemed really nice.

On his Instagram page.

Which wasn't real. Which was made up of carefully curated parts of people's lives designed to look their best.

Her phone chimed.

Another alarm she'd set earlier—this one labeled with "No, Kate You Really Need To Decide!"—had gone off.

"Dammit, woman," she whispered. "Come on. Enough waffling."

Sighing, she stared at herself in the mirror. Red hair, but not a pretty red, boring brown eyes, nice lips—even her critical inner voice had to admit her mouth was great, no doubt her best feature. Lush, perfectly formed, and currently outlined in the perfect shade of red lipstick. Having the skin she did, along with the non-pretty shade of red hair, had made finding that perfect shade of red lipstick a monumental task, and one she'd only found recently, thanks to her friend Heidi and an extremely patient makeup attendant at one of the wall-to-wall beauty stores in the mall.

Twenty-two testers until the Holy Grail had been located.

Firecrotch.

Crude, but perfect.

Some would say that was the perfect description of *her*.

"Ha," she muttered, eyes drifting down the sleek black wrap dress she was wearing. A simple design. It flattered the good parts—boobs, ass—and hid the bad parts—the little pooch below her belly button that never seemed to go away no matter how much hard work she put in at the gym.

Could be that she liked tacos and wine too much, but for the life of her—and it would be a sad, meaningless one if she had to live without tacos and wine—she couldn't give them up.

Crunchy or soft, red or white, boxed or out of the bottle, from Taco Bell or from the legit hole-in-the-wall restaurant around the corner from her apartment.

Her standards were low.

Fill her belly, give her a buzz, and she was golden.

She was also delaying, because she knew what she was going to do. It was why she'd done her makeup, her hair, why she'd gotten dressed and slipped on her favorite heels.

It was Thursday.

Family dinner was tomorrow.

And she wanted to keep that joy in her Mom's tone. Look, she wasn't a saint, she wasn't going to pretend her actions were purely altruistic, but she just wanted to fit in with her family for once.

Not be the odd man out.

Not be the single lady at the couple's party.

She wanted to just . . . be.

Not to mention that Jaime the Vet was hot—a sexy, brown-haired Viking with a man bun that made her jealous, who took care of puppies and kitties and the occasional bearded dragon, based on his pics.

Puppies and kitties and bearded dragons. Who could resist?

Especially when the last picture of a bearded dragon that she'd seen had been wearing a crocheted purple vest.

"I mean, come on," she muttered, turning away from the mirror and picking up her purse. Because for all her prevaricating, the truth was that she'd always been planning on going.

She headed down the hall, toward the front door.

"Okay, Kate McLeod," she said out loud to herself, pausing with her hand on the knob. "This isn't a big deal. First, suss out he's not going to take me home and bury me in his nonexistent basement. *Then* we go to one family dinner together and one Christmas party. After which I fake an implosive fight and we both go on our separate ways." Purse over her arm, firm nod in agreement already halfway complete. "There. Done."

Straightening her shoulders, she tugged open the door and stepped out onto the porch.

Jaime the Vet.

She hoped he came with animals.

HE DID NOT, in fact, come with animals.

He did not, in fact, come at all.

And as she sat at the table by herself, having long ago consumed the entire breadbasket, her heart sinking, her inner critic grew exponentially in volume because . . . *of course* he wouldn't come. She was a strange woman who'd asked via freaking direct message to pretend to be her fiancé for a week.

That was a special brand of psycho.

Men like Jaime the Vet did not voluntarily sign up for that particular brand of cray cray.

Would it have just been nicer for him to ignore her message?

Or to just say no?

Fuck yes, it would have been.

But alas, not all on the Instagram was real, and then there was her superpower—the one that turned nice men into assholes.

It was probably some compulsion she'd woven through the airwaves, a subliminal message hidden in between the letters saying, "Turn into a lying, evil bastard upon reading this message."

Or . . . there could be something in the bread.

Or it could be the third glass of wine.

"Did you want to order?" the nice waitress, who'd been patiently refilling the breadbasket all evening, asked.

Kate sighed, part of her wanting to slink home and feel sorry for herself. The rest of her figured she'd done her hair, put on a dress and heels, was wearing her fancy red lipstick, so yes, she should just order a plate of expensive pasta, another glass of wine, and carbo-load away her happiness.

Hell, she might even live extra vicariously and order a slice of that chocolate cake she'd seen float by on a tray earlier.

"Yes," she said decisively. "I'll have the pasta al pomodoro."

"Me, too."

Lightning.

Like that image from the Marvel movie, Thor lifting his hammer up to the sky, a deluge of electricity exploding from the clouds to coalesce on his weapon.

His voice did that to her.

Collided with her nape, exploded out through her limbs, firing her nerve endings, bringing them to rigid awareness as that deep rumble filled her ears.

"Sorry," the waitress said, sounding a little dazed, and Kate couldn't blame her, not when her cells felt like they'd been lit up like glow sticks at a rave. "What was that?" the waitress asked.

"I'll have what she's having," that sexy male voice said, and Kate was still reeling from it when he moved around the table and sat down in the chair opposite her. "Hi," he murmured, as the waitress nodded and slipped away. Kate barely noticed, not when he was beyond fucking sexy with that rueful smile on his lips. "I'm really sorry I'm late."

Heat. Desire.

That fucking man bun.

Then her mind cleared. Because late? *Late?*

Kate glared over at him and grabbed the last roll, tearing a huge bite off with her teeth. "This is mine," she snapped. Or well, tried to anyway, the words came out muffled. "I can't believe you almost stood me up."

Pale brown eyes dimmed. "Damn. You didn't get my message." He ignored her warning and reached across the table, snagged a piece of the roll. "I'm sorry, Red," he murmured, popping it into his mouth.

Anger gave way to confusion. "Um, what?"

He chewed and swallowed then nodded at her purse. "I'm guessing you didn't check your messages."

As a matter of fact . . . she hadn't.

"There was a complication with my last surgery of the day. I had to stay late, make sure he was okay," he said. "I didn't have your number, so I couldn't call, but I sent you a message on Insta. But when I didn't hear back, saw it seemed like you hadn't read it in the app, I worried you'd be here, and . . ."

"You came to check," she whispered. Confusion gave way to melting.

As in, she went melty inside. Shit.

"I didn't want you to be sitting here alone." His eyes drifted to the empty breadbasket, the drained wineglass. "I see I was too late anyway."

Regret in his tone, those brown eyes soft.

"It's okay," she murmured. "It's my fault. I should have thought to check."

The waitress came back then, two glasses of wine in her hand and another basket. See? She was damned good.

"Thank you," he said, smiling that wide gorgeous smile, and the waitress blinked as she left.

Kate was doing some blinking of her own. He was wearing a nice, but slightly wrinkled, blue button-down and jeans, hair-covered ones if the slight glimpse of his leg she'd gotten held true. There was stubble on his jaw, lines of fatigue surrounding his eyes.

He'd had a long day but still came to check on her.

A stranger.

A good guy.

"Were the complications serious?" she asked, heart twisting. Because she was worried about the animal, not the fact that she might fall for the good guy.

"Not great," he said. "Turns out, the little man has an underlying heart condition. It will take some further steps to determine the cause and follow-up treatment."

"Poor guy," she murmured.

"He's a tough one." Jaime smiled. "But he was soaking up all the extra attention like a champ. When I left, he was trying to crawl into my tech's pocket."

She pushed the bread in his direction, placed her own roll on her plate, pretending she had manners for at least a few moments. Then she asked, "Was the little attention mooch a dog or a cat?"

Must be a small one if he was trying to crawl into pockets.

Maybe a teacup poodle?

Or it could be a non-furry critter, another bearded dragon.

Jaime's lips curved further. "Oh, Hank is a guinea pig. We call him Hank the Tank because he eats like crazy but is really small for his variety." He picked up his roll. "His favorite snacks are kale stems and cantaloupe."

A guinea pig named Hank the Tank, who liked kale and cantaloupe.

"Does he wear a vest?" she asked, heart already squee-ing in anticipation.

"No," Jaime said. "But he does have a tiny bowtie collar."

And *boom*, just like that, her ovaries exploded under the power of squeedom.

THREE

Jaime

HE STARED across the table at a woman he probably should have avoided at all costs.

She'd asked him to participate in a scheme that involved lying to her family. Maybe he could have justified it because who cared, he was lying to people he didn't know, wouldn't know again, but he was a man who preferred honesty.

Had the lying ex once, got the souvenir T-shirt, wasn't going to visit again.

That alone should have been enough ammunition for him to not reply to the message in the first place, let alone agree to the deception.

Except . . . he'd been following *KateMcFunPants* on Instagram for more than a year now.

She was the friend of a friend—apparently worked in the marketing department of Steele Technologies, a large tech company headquartered in San Francisco. His friend, Ben, was friends with Sebastian, a higher-up at the company, and Ben had been photographed with Sebastian and Kate(*McFunPants*) at a few events together. Jaime had been intoxicated first by her mouth, spread wide in a million-dollar smile, then had latched onto her eyes, her curvy body, and he'd followed her. She'd reciprocated, and they'd liked a few of each other's posts—not an obsessive amount going back months and years, but a few here and there.

This was romance in the age of social media, and it was important to use the proper amount of creepage . . . at least publicly.

Because privately?

He'd gone *way* back, far enough to see her feed dotted with more events from Steele Technologies and ex-boyfriends and girls' nights, but he hadn't liked anything from then. He'd been playing the long game—slow and steady, get her comfortable, then boom, swoop in for a date and have her fall for him.

He'd commented on the meme she'd made of fantasy versus reality—in her case a picture of her at goat yoga juxtaposed with one of a model for the company. The half of the meme that featured Kate was an action shot, a goat perched on her head, eating her tank top, as her hands slipped out from beneath her during downward dog. Her expression, along with the goat's, was hilarious, and so far removed from the model's that he'd actually laughed out loud as he'd gotten off BART.

That had earned a few dirty looks in the otherwise quiet train and station, but frankly, the denizens of this city had seen far worse.

She'd liked his comments, and communications had increased.

Date night was in the near future.

At least, that was how it had gone in his head.

But it seemed to be destined to continue that way—remain in his mind and not in real life—unless he got his head out of his ass and pulled the trigger on the whole date thing. The problem was that he was a bit gun shy. Which was the point where his brain circled back to his lying ex and the reason for being gun shy in the first place. They'd originally connected on the 'gram and that had ended . . .

Well, a heat sinking missile had nothing on him and Lori.

Kate was staring up at him with big brown eyes, her long red hair tucked behind one ear, and he was struck again by how pretty she was. And he didn't mean that in a shallow, asshole way, like a woman's worth was only measured in the way she looked. Jaime meant that there was something warm and comforting and just really nice inside her, and it seeped through her smile, shone through those golden-brown eyes, and it felt good to have it directed at him.

Even when she was looking accusingly over her roll at him.

So much so that he found he couldn't resist the urge to tease her. He reached out and snagged another piece of that roll she was so protective of.

"Hey!" she gasped.

He grinned. "I think we missed a few steps."

"Like you eating your *own* roll?" She shoved the basket at him.

"Like me saying, *Hi, Kate, it's nice to meet you*," he said.

She'd sucked in a breath, no doubt to berate him about the roll, but froze when he spoke. Then made a face. It was fucking cute, that little wrinkle over the bridge of her nose. A heartbeat later, it disappeared, her expression smoothing out, and she sighed. "Damn," she said. "We did miss that part, didn't we?"

Jaime shrugged. "Fiancés don't normally need introductions."

Her cheeks colored, but she kept her eyes on his. "You know, you don't have to do this."

Another shrug. "I know."

"Then why *are* you?"

That was the question of the hour, wasn't it?

He hesitated and then figured the best course was to just tell her the truth, albeit a non-stalking of her Instagram profile version of the truth. "You're gorgeous, and you seem nice, and I'd be lying if I said I wasn't hoping to find a way to ask you on a date."

Her mouth dropped open. "You?" A shake of her head. "Me? A date?"

Shit. He hadn't gotten the non-creepy vibe down. Jaime cleared his throat. "Yeah, and well, my family is . . . complicated, and I figured yours must be the same if you were asking, and also that you wouldn't have asked unless you'd gotten pretty far down your list and were getting really desperate."

The roll fell from her hand to the plate. "Desperate?" she parroted.

"Yeah, I mean—" He shrugged. "I'm not exactly—um—" Double shit. He was fucking this up, making it weird. "It's just we're not exactly friends, and . . . well I—"

Cursing inwardly, knowing he wasn't making any sense, Jaime picked up his own roll, cut it in half so he could lather it with butter. When he risked a glance at Kate, he saw she was studying him closely.

"Insecurity knows no bounds, does it?" she said, and it wasn't pity but rather warmth in her eyes. "You were the only person I asked, Jaime. I've been fantasizing about you for months." A self-deprecating shrug. "Well, about you and your adorable little animals you take care of on a daily basis."

Her admission relaxed him, and lips curving, he admitted something he had only told a few close buddies. "I only take pictures with the cute ones. The ugly and mean ones don't merit a selfie."

She smiled at him, and he felt it right in the pit of his stomach. "That's terrible."

He pulled up the sleeve of his shirt. "The ones who scratch me don't get photo ops either."

"Ouch." She reached across the table, brushed her fingers lightly over the injury. The scrapes weren't deep, and while the injury had hurt like hell when it had happened—courtesy of claws from a mean old senior cat with a toothache—the scratches hadn't needed much more than a good cleaning. "Why do you do it?" she asked, pulling her hand back.

"The pictures? Or the animals?" he asked.

"The pictures." A shake of her head paired with a sheepish smile. "Both."

"I'll tell you all," he said, deliberately making his tone sound like one of those late-night psychics. "But I need you to tell me something first." He tilted his head to the side. "Well, no, *two* things."

She ran her fingers through the long red strands of her hair, tucked a few pieces that had come lose back behind her ear. "What are they?"

"First, what's your last name?"

A flash of that pretty, generous smile. "McLeod." A beat. "Yours?"

"Huntington."

She tilted her head to the side. "Fits." A nod. "And the second thing?"

"Was I really the first person you asked?"

Gentle golden-brown eyes, a soft curve to her lips. "Yes, Jaime," she murmured. "The first one. The only one." White teeth closing over a plump red bottom lip. "I wasn't lying before. You're not the only one who's done some Insta fantasizing."

"I—"

But whatever he was going to say—and fuck if he knew what he'd been about to force out—was lost when the waitress set down a plate in front of Kate then an identical one in front of him.

"You guys have everything you need?" she asked.

"Yes, thank you," they said at almost the same time.

The waitress left, and Jaime found himself staring at Kate, the steam from the pasta wafting up and coating his face. But he barely felt it because he couldn't believe she'd asked him first.

They had a connection.

He'd been discounting it because . . . well, social media wasn't real life.

He'd been discounting it because he'd thought that no way could she be into him, not like he was into her.

He'd been discounting it because . . . he'd been off his game for months.

"You didn't answer my question," she said, twining some pasta around her fork.

"Which one?"

"Why you do the whole social media Jaime the Vet thing?"

"Oh." He picked up his own fork. "At first, it was just exciting to have animals to work on, and I wanted to document it. Also"—he grinned, thinking of his mom and her demand for information about his life. She was great, but sometimes needy, and it had been an easy way for her to stay in the loop without having to call her every day—"for my parents. They liked knowing what was up, and it was better than them hounding me about my dating life."

She chuckled as she brought her fork to her mouth, the bite of pasta hitting her tongue, drawing his attention to those plump lips as she chewed and swallowed, a soft moan drifting through the air.

A soft moan that was way too sexy for a first date.

Although . . . not too sexy for a fiancé?

No. Mentally, he smacked himself. Fake fiancé. The keyword being *fake*.

"I know all about families and pushy," she said, pulling him out of all thoughts fake. "I'm the oldest sibling and the only single one. *Oh, the humanity!*" Her lips quirked when she rested the back of her hand on her forehead, *a la* fainting Hollywood starlet of the past. Then she sighed, and a little sad crept into her eyes. "I don't necessarily *want* to be single, but—" She lifted and dropped one shoulder. "Sometimes things don't always work out the way we want."

"I feel that."

A sigh before she set her fork down and then lightly clapped her hands together. "Okay, so here is your last chance to run away or to demand an exorbitant payment in exchange for playing my fake fiancé."

"I thought we covered that already. I'm happy to play your fake fiancé."

Brown eyes narrowed. "Just like that? No ulterior motives, no secret basement with a cabinet full of serial killer tools?"

"Just like that," he said. "And my condo doesn't have a basement."

She began winding pasta around her fork again. "I noticed that you didn't address the ulterior motive piece of my statement."

A snort. "I already told you I wanted a date." He waved a hand at the table, the plates, the glasses of wine. "Thus, my ulterior motive satisfied."

"Hmm."

She put the bite into her mouth, and he took the opportunity to do the same. The pasta was good, great even, but he could barely taste it. Not when his focus was so firmly on the woman across from him. Fascinating. Beautiful. Empathetic. Nice.

And quiet.

Just a little quiet, as though she didn't mind short stretches of silence.

It was nice, that quiet. Peaceful, not oppressive. *She* was nice.

She set her fork down, eyes going wide, and he felt a blip of alarm travel through him. "What?" he asked.

"I just realized that if we're doing this, there is so much I need to brief you on. My family. My parents. My siblings—"

"That's the definition of family, right?" he teased.

"Shush, you," she said, though her smile was teasing the corners of her lips up. "But also, yes, I guess that's what I meant by family."

"Can't we play it by ear?" he asked. "It's only two dinners."

"They're going to interrogate you." She groaned. "They're going to want all the details of how we met and our first date and—oh God!—my friends. You haven't met my friends. They don't know anything about you, and they know *everything*." She picked up her fork, shoved a bite of pasta into her mouth, all while shaking her head fiercely. Once she'd swallowed, she shook her head firmly once more, scattering her hair over her shoulders. "We can't do this. *I* can't do this. It's insanity. I just need to come clean."

He didn't want her to come clean. He *wanted* more time with her. "It's two dinners."

"I—"

He shrugged. "I can manage two dinners, Kate."

"You haven't met my family."

Laughter bubbled up in his chest. "Ditto." He reached across the table, squeezed her hand. "How about you pretend two dinners are my ulterior motive?"

She frowned.

"Two more dates," he explained. "That aren't family

dinners. That are just you and me getting to know one another. *That* will be payment for your favor."

"Deception with a side of ulterior?"

His lips twitched. "Seems fitting, yeah?"

"Yeah," she agreed. "Or maybe it's dinner with a side of engagement?"

The laughter didn't just bubble up this time, it burst right out of him. "Yes," he said through it. "That's exactly it."

"Damn." She made a face.

His amusement cut off. "What?"

"You're even nicer than I expected."

"Is that a bad thing?"

"Only that"—she shook her head—"never mind, it's a silly thought."

"No." His hand found hers again. "What is it?"

A forkful of pasta into her mouth, her words muffled. "Really," she said, "it doesn't matter."

"We can't start off a fake engagement on a lie."

Her mouth fell open, a strangled sound emerging. "What? That doesn't even make sense."

"Sure, it does." He snagged her roll again, brought it up to his mouth like he was going to eat it, and her gasp of outrage made it clear that was the best ransom around. "Tell me," he ordered.

She frowned. "So, sexy, smart, funny, nice, rocks a perfect man bun, and also a blackmailer."

"Fiancés should discover these things about each other." He shrugged, forced himself to bite back his smile when she rolled her eyes. "See, Red? We've made progress in our deception."

She snagged the much-abused roll back. "Mine." A bite. "And also, I was thinking that nice never lasts, okay?" She took another bite, chewed and swallowed, deliberately changing the subject. "Okay, so I'm the oldest of three. What about you? How many siblings do you have?"

Jaime knew he had a choice. Push or let it go.

Pushing might destroy the fragile bond they were just beginning to build. Pushing might mean he'd never get to his other plans—that being, how to get more than two dates with this smart, lovely woman sitting across from him. Pushing might mean that he'd never get a chance to turn fake into real.

So, he let it go.

And then he told her about his family.

FOUR

Kate

HE'D PAID THE BILL, like it was a legitimate date.

He'd talked about his family with equal parts love and exasperation. That was such a familiar feeling and one that made her like him even more.

It made him dangerous, the degree with which she liked him, and yet she also wanted to live in the moment, wanted to grasp on to that floating feeling of a new relationship.

When everything was all puppy dogs and rainbows and fun.

Before it deteriorated and the asshole appeared.

"Can I—?" She blinked out of her woolgathering, saw that Jaime was gesturing at her hand, asking to hold it.

Her ovaries were already dead and gone from one bowtie wearing guinea pig and kind brown eyes, and now her heart spasmed.

Fuck, he was nice.

She nodded, and he laced his fingers with hers. Such a simple touch, but it still took her breath away. His hand engulfed hers, the sensation from the roughness of his palm rubbing against the softness of hers. It raised the hairs on her arm, made heat drift down her spine, slid in—

"Your fingers are cold," he murmured, wrapping his other hand around hers and bringing it up to his mouth, blowing warm air over her skin.

She shivered.

"That's not all that's cold," he said, dropping her hand and shrugging out of his jacket. He dropped it over her shoulders, covering the thin wrap she'd donned but that didn't do much to protect her from the cool evening air. "As much as I hate to cover up that pretty dress," he whispered in her ear, "I can't have you turning into a popsicle." Then slipped an arm around her waist and tugged her against his side.

Being there, pressed against the hard of his muscles, the spicy male scent surrounding her, his arm a hot brand around her middle, meant it took a few moments for her to whisper, "I wasn't actually cold. I just like the way your hand feels against mine."

A soft admission. One she almost couldn't believe she'd spoken aloud.

But then again, nothing about this entire scenario was believable.

He didn't say anything for a moment. "Are you too hot now?"

She shook her head.

"Then it's win-win for both of us."

Smiling, she snuggled closer, and when he asked if she wanted to walk down to the waterfront, she agreed even though her feet were killing her. "Why does it feel like I've known you for more than one date?" she blurted.

His fingers tightened on her waist. "Because we're fake engaged?"

Kate snorted. "Somehow I doubt that's it."

"Because you're really into me?" he teased.

"I'm really into your Instagram profile, that's for sure," she teased back. "All of those animals." A shrug. "And I guess that fact that you're in them too is fine."

He tickled her lightly. "I feel the same."

She tapped her chin, teasing aside, it was a legitimate thought. She never felt this comfortable with men after just a few hours. There was just something about Jaime that made her feel like she'd arrived home. "Maybe it's because we're both part of big families?"

"Big, *nosy* families?"

"Yeah, that, too. Wait. Come this way," she said, pointing to a walkway when he was going to miss the best part of this area. After they'd rounded the building and slid into a little alcove that overlooked the perches where the sea lions liked to rest during the day, but for now was beautifully illuminated by the bright moon overhead, she said, "Well, either way, I'm just really thankful that you agreed to my scheme. I know it's wrong to lie to my parents, but I just want . . ."

Ick. It made her sound like a total wimp to admit that she didn't want to disappoint them. But . . . it was the truth. She'd disappointed them far too often in her life.

"When your family is close, it's hard to feel like you're not meeting their expectations."

A sigh. "Yeah. That."

And also, maybe *that* was the fact that this man had led her over to a bench and was cuddling her close.

Because *that* was incredible.

Big body. Warm hands. Intoxicating smell. Gentle words. Soft hold.

Jaime was a cornucopia of her fantasies come to life.

"What else should a fake fiancé know about his woman?" he asked when they sat in quiet for a couple of minutes.

Kate thought for a few seconds. "Her favorite color is purple. She likes sunflowers and loves Hermione Granger. She can't stand tomatoes but loves all things marinara and ketchup." She nudged his shoulder. "How about you? What should I know about my fake significant other? Besides his amazing blackmail abilities and his abuse of my roll."

A grin that hit her right in the gut, his voice close to her ear and making her shiver all over again. "Well, his favorite color is red. He's partial to dogs over cats and will eat anything as long as he can drown it in ketchup."

She fist-pumped. "Ketchup buddies."

"I can see it now," he said, spreading the hand that wasn't resting on her waist wide as though he were a director painting the scene for his actors. And maybe he was, for all that she'd had fun the last few hours, the crux of what was between them *was* just acting. "We fell in love at first sight when we both reached for the same ketchup bottle at the diner."

"Our hands touched." She reached out, squeezed his fingers, forced herself to keep her tone light. "And sparks flew."

His voice dropped, a silken thread sliding across the back of her neck. "And that was it for me," he murmured, tugging her closer and resting his chin on the top of her head. "I somehow convinced you to give me your number. The rest is history."

A blip of disappointment slid through her. Not because she didn't like the story, but because she liked it too much.

"Exactly," she said, straightening, sliding from his hold, and pushing to her feet. "But we should get going. I have to work at least half a day tomorrow."

"About that," he said. "What time is dinner? Should I pick you up so we can drive together?"

She nodded. "Yes. That sounds good. Dinner is at seven-thirty, but we should try to be there by about six-thirty. Want to pick me up at my place? It's only a half hour drive, even with Friday traffic."

"I can do that." He pushed to his feet, reached for her hand. "I'll be there at six and we can drive over."

"You sure?" Kate asked. "Last chance to run screaming for the hills."

"I'm sure."

"You don't have any temperamental cats on the schedule?"

He grinned and she melted from the inside out, letting him tug her to her feet, reveling in the feel of his warm, rough palm against hers. This might all be pretend, but there was one thing that wasn't fake—the way her body responded. She enjoyed the contact, felt comfortable with him touching her. Okay, so *more* than comfortable. She freaking loved it, wanted to strip off his clothes and see if his abs were as good as his pictures, wanted to feel the strands of his hair brushing across her stomach as he kissed his way down.

A shiver, even with his coat.

"Come on," he murmured. "Let's get you out of the cold."

Not about to confess why she'd shivered this time, Kate leaned close when he wrapped his arm around her waist, walked beside him as they made their way back to her car. "So, no cats?" she asked, after he'd inquired about where she was parked, and had turned them in the direction of it with the confidence of someone who'd lived in the city for a long time.

"Maybe one or two," he said, tracing. "But I definitely have a temperamental chicken."

Her feet skidded to a halt and she tugged him to a stop. When pale brown eyes drifted down to hers, she placed her hand on his chest in a movement that felt natural and yet also far too intimate. But when she made as though to pull back, he placed his palm over her fingers, pressed lightly to keep her hand there.

Her pulse fluttered, but she forced herself to say, "Explain."

The ghost of a smile. "About the chicken?"

She huffed. "Obviously."

"I'll tell you as we walk," he said, urging her forward.

Narrowing her eyes in mock-warning, she started moving again. "You'd better. What's the temperamental chicken's name?"

"Barry."

Her feet threatened to stop again, but his arm just tightened, hand coaxing her forward. "Tut. Tut. No stopping. My woman is cold."

Another shiver, this one caused not by her brain and its fantasies, but by the notes of heat beneath that phrase *my woman*. In another world. In her dreams. In a fake lie that . . .

"Well, my *man* doesn't give orders," she countered.

He burst out laughing. "Maybe more accurate would be to say that my woman doesn't listen to orders."

She chuckled. "That would be the truth."

"So, you want to hear about Barry the Chicken?"

"That may be my favorite question that anyone has ever asked me."

He snorted. "Is that a yes?"

Her fingers tightened on his chest, pressing against his skin, feeling the steady *thrum-thrum* of his heart beneath. "That's a yes." She grinned up at him, rising on tiptoe, wanting to see his face clearly when he told her the story. Except, she miscalculated and lost her balance, falling against him, her breasts pressed to his chest.

She gasped, nipples hardening, fingers clenching. "Jaime—"

In a move so quick that she could barely process it, she suddenly found her back pressed against the cool stucco of the building they were walking next to. He'd slid an arm behind her back, cushioning her against the hardness of the wall, and his body was pressed to hers, so hot, so hard, surrounding her, over-whelming her, making her head spin, her nipples ache, her thighs quiver.

"I want to kiss you."

It wasn't phrased as a question, but rather a statement. As thus, it took her a moment to process his words, especially with him all warm and hard against her.

"Okay," she whispered.

His mouth was on hers.

No hesitation. No long, slow descent.

One second she was pushing the assent out of her lips, the next, his tongue was in her mouth, stroking along hers, his free hand on her cheek, angling her head so he could taste her properly.

It was a whirlwind, that kiss.

Not gentle or teasing. Not like a typical first date peck.

This was domination. This surrounded her, took her over, filled her with fire that threatened to incinerate her from the inside out.

Then it was done.

He shifted back minutely, slid the hand on her face down her arm, her side, resting it on her hip. But he kept his body against hers, and the feel of him was enough to take her breath away. "Want to hear about Barry the Chicken?"

Her fingers were in his hair, mussing the neatly organized locks when they clenched at the husky question. "No."

One eyebrow lifted. "No?"

Kate rose onto her tiptoes. "No," she murmured. "*I'd* rather kiss *you*."

And then she put words to action.

Luckily, Jaime didn't seem to mind.

FIVE

Jaime

IT HAD BEEN a spectacular first date.

And he'd been engaged for the entirety of it.

Snorting, he made a few notes in the computer and thought of the snap he'd sent to Kate a few hours earlier, beyond glad he'd managed to finagle her number from her.

Well, in all honesty, it was less finagling and more common sense.

Fiancés had their future wives' numbers.

Simple as that.

Except . . . nothing was simple when it came to this woman and the depth of feeling he had for her after one dinner and a short walk. Maybe it was all the social media stalking, or maybe it was just her, just the realization and fleshing out of that feeling he'd had upon seeing that first picture.

The notion deep inside that this woman was more than just a face in a photograph.

Now he had a chance to prove that to himself . . . or maybe to her . . . or the universe, her parents, her siblings, and friends.

Long ass list, that was.

But the thought of lying to everyone important to her, and the unease it caused, had slipped way to the back of his brain. Because when he was in her presence, the only important thing was getting closer, unearthing all the little—and big, he supposed—things that made Kate, Kate.

Like the GIF and chain of emojis she'd replied with after he'd sent her a picture of him and Barry.

He'd never actually seen that many emojis in a row and had spent a good amount of time going one by one before he'd been able to translate the gist of the message.

And when he'd texted back

Please spare the old man so many emojis. It took me way too long to figure that out.

She'd simply replied with another chain of the tiny pictures. Though at least he'd been able to deduce the meaning of the hearts and kissing face emoji and had replied with

I like kissing you, too.

Long minutes had passed before he'd seen actual words.

You really don't use emojis.

Is this an emoji? :)

A beat

Nope.

Then. Nope, I guess I don't.

Hmm.

Do I need to read up on emoji etiquette?

Only if you want to understand my messages.

He'd laughed out loud at that but then had needed to slip his cell into his pocket and get down to work, otherwise he wouldn't have a hope in hell of getting out of the clinic on time.

Jaime had focused on getting through his patients, on returning calls and following up on lab work, but when he was on lunch break, he'd downloaded an *Emojis for Dummies Guidebook,* screenshotting the cover and sending it to Kate, along with a message.

Prepping for my crash course.

She'd replied almost instantly.

Smart. *thinking emoji*

(see, he'd already learned something)
Then

You said, you're an old man. How old exactly? I may need to rethink my plan.

Snorting, he shoved a bite of salad into his mouth and typed back.

Thirty-two. Birthday is August 2nd. You?

A long, long silence.

Don't you know that's an impolite question?

Don't you know that fiancés know these things? *sad eye emoji*

And okay, now he saw that the tiny and weird little pictures might truly be worthwhile, especially when her reply came through.

Not the sad eyes. Dear God, my heart can't take the sad eyes.

Noted. *another sad eye emoji* *Now, tell me. Please?*

I'm alternating between sighing out loud and giggling in my cube, and my coworkers think I've gone crazy.

He frowned.

Didn't you eat lunch?

No time today. Not if I want to be on time. I've got a big project that's due. Note the deliberate use of *sad face emoji* *in payback to you.*

Turns out, I'm immune. How old, Red? Then I'll let you go.

eye roll emoji *Thirty-two, but the painful truth is that my birthday is July 22nd.*

Jaime grinned.

So less old man and more old woman?

*Blasphemy! *cursing emoji**

The tech came in as he was laughing and told him his next patient was there, and he quickly shoved the last bite of his salad into his mouth.

*I know. It's terrible. *sad eye emoji* That's so you'll forgive me. But I'd better let you work.*

Unfortunately, yes.

A beat before another message came through.

I like texting with you, Jaime the Vet.

He could imagine her looking up shyly as she said that, the same way she'd looked up and said *No, I'd rather kiss you* the previous night, right before she tugged him down and kissed him within an inch of his sanity.

I like it, too, Red. See you in a few hours.

A chain of hearts and flowers and strange little yellow faces was his only reply, but it turned out that he quite liked emojis, especially when a gorgeous little redhead with curves for days and pretty whiskey-colored eyes sent them to him.

Sparing another minute before pulling his lab coat back on and heading to the exam room to see one of his temperamental feline patients, he opened the app on his phone and ordered lunch to be delivered to Kate's office.

He knew her favorite meal. Or at least one that had been featured on her Instagram page more than once—a pear and walnut salad and an apple turnover.

See? His social media spying had paid off. He knew where she worked and what food she liked and her favorite beach and—

Pausing, because that sounded creepy, even in his own head, he forced himself to focus and completed the order for a salad and pastry from Molly's, a city staple that made even the healthiest of meals taste good.

Not that the pastry was healthy, but he figured Kate deserved a treat, especially when paired with the green stuff, and anyone who was anyone got a pastry when they ordered from Molly's. Handmade every day by the owner, plumb full of deliciousness, someone would have to be an idiot to not pick one up, especially given how often Kate waxed poetic about them on her page.

Not that he didn't agree, but the fact that it was another piece of information from her social media was probably semi-creepy. Regardless, he was chalking it up to paying attention to key details about a woman he wanted to win over.

Pastries. Not a bad way to start, he could imagine his sister, Tammy, telling him.

And, considering he'd been well-trained, Jaime knew his instincts on that front were right at least. He might have fucked up with Lori and had his confidence dinged, but he knew after one date with Kate that she was one hundred percent different from his ex.

She teased but in a sweet way. She'd fought him over the bill (though he'd won, Jaime thought with a self-satisfied smirk). She'd leaned into his touch, rather than shying away.

Lori had been beautiful, but with a streak of mean. She'd never offered to pay, had hated if he wanted to hold her hand in public.

Silly, small things. Well, not the mean, but the rest of it hadn't been obvious at first, or at least not enough to have propelled him into ending things. But then again, Lori had been good at manipulating him, good at giving him just enough affection that he clambered after her, wanting more, starved for more contact, more time with her.

Look, he understood her wanting to have her own life. He was independent, himself.

But he wanted more in a relationship.

He wanted a partner, someone he could share funny news stories or memes or inside jokes with. He craved a connection that didn't have him second-guessing every motivation and undercurrent.

Which was why it had been almost refreshing to get the message from Kate.

Will you pretend to be my fiancé for a week?

No subterfuge. No hiding.

Just a request and an in—a way for him to get closer to the fascinating woman he'd been lusting over.

He was mercenary enough to take it, selfish enough to want to tie her to him, smart enough to know that if he had any chance of success that he'd need to utilize a charm offensive the world had never seen before.

One glance, and he'd known that she was special.

One night, and he'd known he was hooked on the drug that was Kate.

So, he had a plan. A plan that involved several errands after he was done with his clients.

Speaking of which, a bark in the room next to him startled Jaime into motion. He shook himself, put away his phone, hurried to clean up his lunch. Because yes, he had a plan to make Kate fall for him, but that plan would only work if he didn't actually fuck up this fake fiancé role.

And the first step in that was being on time.

SIX

Kate

IT WAS 5:56 and she was pacing back and forth along the narrow entryway of her house south of San Francisco.

One side had an opening to a small kitchen.

The other opened up into an equally small living room, packed with her too big but cozy microfiber couch. It was soft. It was fluffy. It was a deep, deep shade of violet, and she loved it most of all her belongings.

In fact, she loved it as much as she loved the back yard.

And that had taken blood, sweat, and tears to get to its current state. Though, she supposed, the couch had also taken blood and sweat to get it in through the narrow hall. But no tears. Plenty of cursing, especially from her brother and dad, who'd helped her move in, but no tears.

She'd smiled at the memory.

Her parents were so damned proud that she'd managed to scrimp and save enough to buy a house in the competitive Bay Area housing market, her mom only making one comment about how she could sell when she met her future husband because *surely, he would want to be part of the house-buying-decision-making process* that Kate had been able to easily ignore.

She loved her mom, but damn, could that woman be a dog to the bone.

Still, she had inherited her green thumb from her mom and grandma, her taste in clothing that had notes of trendy but had given her the skills to build a wardrobe with classic, tasteful pieces that had lasted years.

Like the dress Jaime hadn't been able to tear his eyes off last night.

That was one of her favorites—sexy, flattered her curves, showed just the right amount of tits and ass to make her appetizing but not cross that line into nip slip.

Tits and ass?

Clearly, she'd been watching too much bad reality TV, because that particular vernacular had never been in her vocabulary until she'd begun watching a behind the scenes reality show of strippers and their personal lives.

Most of the time, reality TV was fascinating.

Sometimes her consumption habits reminded her that perhaps she needed to throw in a documentary every once in a while, in order to balance out the brain-melting. Still, it was a guilty pleasure, and one she couldn't feel *too* guilty for, given that Kate was in advertising. She found people and their habits fascinating.

What she *didn't* find fascinating was the amount of nerves currently swirling around her stomach.

She should call it off.

But then she'd miss out on spending the night with Jaime, miss out on his sweet, miss out on the way he'd held her hand, and how he'd kissed her until she thought that her clothes might just melt off into a puddle, not giving one damn that they were on a public street and anyone might see them.

Public indecency charge? Meh.

She'd had Jaime the Vet's lips on hers, his body pressed against hers, his fingers on her jaw, his tongue in her mouth.

Yeah. Indecency charges would have been worth it.

But eventually he'd released her mouth, had cuddled her close to his side, and had walked her to her car. She'd been enshrouded in a haze of desire, one she'd wanted to hold on to tightly because it was so potent, but one she'd been forced to pull herself out of because she needed to identify her car.

He'd made it easier by telling her about Barry the Chicken.

Who was apparently a rooster, but his original owner hadn't known that until she'd ended up with a series of very loud, very abrupt early mornings.

Barry had been rehomed and his current owner lived on a small patch of land with much more understanding neighbors and a love for being up when the sun rose. She'd trained Barry to walk on a leash, and her feisty, feathered companion had become a regular at the clinic.

A rooster named Barry who walked on a leash.

"The man is kryptonite."

Shaking her head, she gave herself one final glance in the mirror she kept inside her hall closet for just this case—a last-minute outfit check—smoothed a nonexistent wrinkle out of her pretty emerald green fit-and-flare dress, slipped on her flats, and then slicked on one more coat of her Firecrotch.

Heh.

Never got old.

Eyes flicking to the clock and seeing it was a minute until six, she grabbed her coat but didn't put it on because she wanted Jaime to see her in the dress. Smiling and hoping he'd like it as much as the black one from the night before, she closed the closet door.

Ding. Dong.

Her pulse skittered, speeding up, butterflies emerging from their cocoons to fly in circles in her stomach, her lips and fingertips tingling in anticipation.

"Okay," she murmured. "It'll be okay."

She strode to the door and pulled it open.

Then blinked and felt her jaw drop open.

"Oh my God, your *hair*," she moaned, reaching up before stopping herself. Because the man bun was *gone*.

Why was the man bun gone?

He smiled, and she saw he'd shaved off the stubble, too, revealing a strong, clean line that she wanted to run her lips across. "You don't like it?" he asked, rubbing a hand over the shorn locks on the side of his head.

Oh, she liked it.

She liked it a hell of a lot.

But the man bun was gone, and she hadn't even really gotten to run her fingers through it or learned how he made his messy bun look so much better than hers.

"I figured I'd better clean up for your parents," he said. "They seem a bit traditional, and I was more than tired of it, just had been too lazy to get a haircut." A blip of uncertainty flittered across his face. "Did I mess up?"

Her heart squeezed, and she closed the distance between them, running her fingers lightly through the brown locks, not messing them up, but rather giving in to her urge to touch the silky softness.

"No," she murmured. "You look too handsome by half."

His lips turned up. "You trying to charm me?"

A shrug, her tone bordering on grandiose. "I speak but the truth."

Jaime tucked a strand of her hair behind her ear. "Are you going Shakespeare on me?"

"Well," she said. "You *are* looking at the famous Lady

Macbeth from Sierra High School's production of Macbeth in 2004. I'll have you know that I got not one but two standing ovations for my performance."

"I'm thoroughly impressed."

She giggled and started to shrug into her coat, breath catching when he grabbed it from her and helped her slide it on. "I didn't get a chance to thank you," she murmured, heart pounding when he gathered her hair at her nape and freed it from the collar of her coat. "For lunch. That was very sweet of you."

A brush of his lips across the back of her neck before he released her hair. "You have time to eat it?"

"Food from Molly's?" she said. "I made time." Spinning around, she decided that she would spend the night not second-guessing and hoping that things between them were different, but instead she'd just enjoy being with this man who was nice and sweet and seemed to like her.

Rising on tiptoe, she pressed a kiss to his lips.

And just like last night, pleasure exploded through her, shutting off her brain so she wasn't thinking or worrying or riddled with guilt. Rather, for the first time in a long time, Kate was able to just be in the present.

His lips moving on hers, his hand cupping her cheek. The spicy male scent of him surrounding her and going to her head more than a glass of wine.

They kissed until her lungs threatened to explode, and then she dropped back down onto her feet, pulling her mouth from his, her heart beating out of control. Her chest rose and fell rapidly, and her lipstick was all over his mouth.

"Shit," she muttered. "I Firecrotched you."

He'd started to smile, to say something, but then it seemed that her words processed because his mouth dropped open. *"What?"*

Which was the moment she realized that this man wasn't privy to the color of her lipstick. Because his gaze dropped down, scorching a path to . . . well, her fire—

Yeah, no.

"It's the name of my lipstick," she rushed to say, lifting a hand and rubbing it over his mouth. "I'm sorry. I got it all over you."

A wicked gleam in his eyes, a warm palm on her back, trailing up and down, up and down. "You're apologizing because you Firecrotched me." Laughter bubbling in his chest, his fingers wrapping around her hip.

"Fine," she said, stepping back and mock-frowning. "I won't apologize." She reached for her purse, snagging it from the small table she kept near the door, where she'd set it when she started putting on her coat, and caught a glimpse of the time. "Crap." They'd been making out in her hall for almost ten minutes. "We need to get moving." She made a pitstop to touch up her lipstick, opening the closet door and using the mirror to slick on a fresh coat, then turned and glared. "No more kissing with that non-scruffy mouth of yours. It's too distracting."

He grinned. "So, you like the haircut and the shave?"

She just kept her narrowed gaze on him. "It's unfair that you're so pretty." A sniff. "And that you had better hair than me when it was long."

"I dream about your hair spread over my pillow at night."

Silence.

As in *she* went silent.

"What?"

"You're so fucking beautiful," he murmured, coming up behind her, running his fingers through her hair, which she'd left loose to trail over her shoulders. "Your hair is the color of rubies. I couldn't believe it when I saw it shining in the restaurant. I always thought it was a filter, that it couldn't be real. But I was wrong." He bent his head and inhaled. "Roses. Roses and rubies and silk."

Goose bumps prickled on her skin, and she melted back against him, the line of her spine colliding with the hard planes of his chest, his abs. "Have you ever felt this way with another person?" she asked.

"No." A stroke of those fingers over her collarbones. "Only with you. From the moment I first saw your picture, I knew you were different."

Her breath shuddered out.

She'd felt that way, too, had become almost obsessed with seeing his posts, but she also knew that her personality bordered on obsessive, that she was always falling too far, too fast, too soon.

This was too soon.

So, instead of saying what was in her heart, she pulled back.

Gently, and with a joke, but she still pulled back. "So, the man who knows nothing of emojis, knows about filters?"

He seemed to understand she needed the distance because he let her go, also stepping back, his soft chuckle filling the air, gentle now without a hint of sexual tension, then reached for the doorknob. "I *had* to learn about them, or at least that was what my vet tech told me when I started the page last year. I quote *couldn't look shiny.*" He opened the door. "And I shouldn't say I know *nothing* about emojis, I've been known to use one of those ones that's suggested when you type."

She snorted, followed him out onto her porch, and took a few moments to lock up.

"I should have asked," she said when they were on their way to his car, a mid-sized black SUV parked in her driveway, "was I on your way? I could have come and picked you up instead."

"I'm not far," he said and gave her the address of his condo, which was actually just in the next neighborhood over. Then he opened the passenger door and helped her in.

"Wait." She grabbed his hand, finally processing that he lived in a condo. She'd imagined . . . what? A farm or a big house with a back yard filled with animals. He couldn't have that in a condo.

Shit. *Shit.* Why had she spent all that time kissing him instead of peppering him with questions? She didn't know nearly enough to pull off this ruse.

"What, Red?" he asked, turning his hand so he could wrap his fingers around her wrist.

"Do you have any pets?"

He shook his head. "No," he said. "Not since my Honey died last year. I . . . sometimes it's hard to be around animals all day, especially when you see them in pain far too often." Fingers on her cheek. "I know I'll get another dog or cat someday, but I just needed some time."

"I'm sorry," she said, reaching out and running her thumb along his jaw, hating the shadow of pain in his eyes. "That must be hard, seeing all those sick animals. I guess, I just had this image it was all . . . kittens and puppies."

"Those are definitely the fun days," he said, voice still soft. "And I love my job, most of the time. It's like anything else and has it's tough moments."

She shook her head. "Except when *I* mess up on an ad mockup, there isn't anyone's life at risk."

Pale brown eyes on hers, filled with so much warmth that she actually felt her heart expand. "True," he said. "But that pressure is part of the job."

"And what do you do to release that pressure?"

He froze. Then he sighed and admitted, "Not enough recently, that's for sure. When I took over the clinic, I knew the hours would be long, but they've been intense and a little overwhelming."

She wrapped her arms around him, held him tight. "I can only imagine."

"Thank you," he murmured. "For asking. And for giving me my first break from the clinic in months with dinner last night," he added, brushing a kiss to her forehead before straightening and reaching to close the car door. Then, as she was beginning to understand was his M.O., this man turned the topic off himself and back onto her. "You know, we don't have to do this. I could go as your boyfriend or just as your date. You could just say your mom misheard or that you made a mistake."

So tempting.

And yet, then she'd have to see the disappointment on her mom's face.

Plus, "What am I going to say?" she asked honestly. "That I thought you had a ring and I was wrong?"

A flicker of humor on his face. "I—"

"Oh shit."

"What?"

She lifted her left hand. Her ring*less* left hand. *Fuck.* She hadn't thought of a ring. *Why* hadn't she thought of a ring? There was no way her mom would believe she'd gotten engaged without a ring. Which, she got, made her sound like a materialistic prima donna, but engagements and rings went hand in hand. If Kate was planning on getting married, she would have a ring.

Except . . . she *didn't* have a ring.

"What, Red?" he asked again, but not impatiently. Instead, those brown eyes stayed gentle, his fingers on her wrist snug, but not tight. His thumb rubbed patterns on the palm of her right hand.

"I don't have a ring." She shook her head. "I should have thought to get a ring—"

"I have one," he said simply and dropped her hand to reach into his pocket and retrieve a box. It was blue velvet, and when he opened the top, she gasped. "Not a real diamond," he murmured. "I didn't think you'd—" A sharp shake of his head. "Anyway, it's called a moonstone, and I thought it was pretty and unique and . . . you. But you can always just tell them it's a temporary ring because I wanted you to be able to pick out what you wanted."

She ran a finger over the soft white stone. It was diamond-esque, but opaque with translucent streaks of sky blue. She'd never seen anything quite like it.

She also thought it the prettiest ring she'd ever seen.

"You did this all today?" she asked. "The lunch, the ring, the haircut, and shaving. All of it . . . for me?"

Jaime brushed the back of his knuckles over her cheek. "It was nothing," he said. "And even if it were, you're worth it, Red. It took no time at all for me to recognize that fact, honey, and if any man was stupid enough to not recognize that, then it was his loss and my gain." He slipped the ring from the box. "Because I intend to get many more than just my two dates." He snagged her left hand, bringing it toward him, and fitting the ring just over the tip of the proper finger. "Got it?"

Her heart pounded, hope filling her with so much helium that she felt as though she could float. Still, she shook her head. "I think we're insane. This is too much and . . . just idiotic. I know it was my idea, but—"

He kissed her briefly then pulled back.

A wicked smile as he slipped the ring down her finger then lifted his hand and ran his thumb over her bottom lip. "Then let's be idiotic together."

SEVEN

Jaime

SHE'D GIVEN him quiet but clear directions to her parents' house, and even with their slight delay in the hall, at the car, and the Friday evening traffic, they still arrived only just after six-thirty.

An old ranch-style house set into the side of rolling hills, green this time of year after the early winter rains, but not yet dried to brown by the dryness of late spring and the summer's heat, it was a beautiful piece of architecture with a wrap-around porch surrounded by lush flowerbeds. The double front doors were stained a rich brown, and a festive Christmas wreath hung centered over each wooden panel.

"You grew up here?" he asked, the gorgeous home so different, so much grander than his own upbringing had provided.

"No," she said. "We grew up in a much smaller house. We moved because—" A shrug. "My mom invented a product that got patented when I was in high school."

That was unusual enough that he managed to tear his gaze from the perfectly straight Christmas lights framing each window, from the family of light-up deer "grazing" on the perfect green lawn. Then again, everything about this woman was interesting, including this house and what it said about her. "What did your mom invent?"

"She's a scientist," Kate said. "Or was. She invented an anti-aging compound, sold it off to the highest bidder, and that became my parents' retirement." She smiled. "Good thing, too. Since my younger siblings seemed determined to eat them out of house and home."

"Excuse me!" a female voice exclaimed. "I'm not the only one who ate." She held up an infant. "Did you hear that, Lacy? Your aunt called me fat."

Kate grinned. "You look beautiful, and you know it." She slipped past Jaime to hug the woman he presumed was her sister, Ann. "In fact, I should hate you, considering you're one of those formerly pregnant females who bounce right back into shape."

A rueful smile. "Believe me," she said. "All sorts of things are bouncing that shouldn't be bouncing."

"Well," Kate said, scooping the baby out of her arms. "I stand by my statement"—she kissed each of the little girl's tiny, plump cheeks—"your mommy is absolutely beautiful. Are you letting her get any sleep yet?"

"Nope." A twinkling laugh. "So, you going to introduce me to the man who you managed to keep a secret for all these months?"

"Not tough with everything that has been going on."

"True enough." She turned to Jaime, stuck her hand out. "Since this one"—she poked her sister in the shoulder—"isn't going to be polite, I've got to take matters into my own hands. I'm Ann."

"I know," he said, smiling and shaking her hand. "I'm Jaime.

Kate has told me a lot about you, including the fact that you're her favorite sister."

"Her only sister is more like it," Ann said with a laugh. "But one she's stuck with." She leaned over and grinned at Kate. "I see you've got yourself a charmer."

Kate grinned back.

"Here." Jaime snagged the diaper bag from her shoulder. "Let me carry that for you."

A raised eyebrow before she laced her arm through his. "Thank you," she said then smiled up at him. "Though I have to say that Kate has been surprisingly tight-lipped about *you*."

He shrugged. "Sometimes it's nice to have something that just belongs to you for a bit."

Ann's smile didn't dim. In fact, it seemed to grow larger, or at least more approving. "Well, I hope you enjoyed that time while it lasted because you'd better believe that an interrogation is coming tonight."

Just as she finished the sentence, the front door opened and an older female waved excitedly, calling, "Come in already!"

Kate groaned.

And it turned out that Ann was right about the interrogation.

A hockey game was on TV, the Gold decimating their opponent, thanks to the outstanding play of Liam Williamson, but Jaime couldn't concentrate on the screen, not when he had four eyes boring holes in his profile.

An unexpected consequence of him being "engaged" to Kate was the fact that he hadn't considered that this engagement had happened without meeting her family.

Or more specifically, without meeting her father, who had

ice in his brown eyes identical to Kate's, or her brother, who had the red hair but a pair of piercing blue irises that were sharp enough to cut.

His "fiancé" had been swept into the kitchen approximately thirty seconds after her mother, a thin brunette with pale blue eyes, had barreled down the front walk, introduced herself as Marabelle McLeod. She'd bustled them into the house then waved him in the direction of the family room, telling him to make himself "at home."

He'd hesitated in the entrance, glanced toward the two men seated on the couch, and then had said, "Hi. I'm Jaime."

Grunts in response.

Which was the moment that he'd realized this was going to be slightly more complicated than he'd anticipated.

Considering his options, he'd sat in an armchair, had trained his focus on the television, and tried to put himself in their place. A man they'd never met, a stranger had asked their daughter/sister to marry him without ever meeting her family. Wincing, he knew that wasn't exactly the first impression he'd wanted to make, especially because he really liked Kate, had felt that instant connection click into place over dinner, had been drawn in further by the walk, by the text conversations, even just chatting on the car ride over. It felt . . . right.

As though he'd been doing his whole life wrong until Kate had messaged him.

"We're having a long engagement," he blurted, turning to look at the two men who'd been staring him down for the last ten minutes. Jaime saw the blip of surprise on their faces, kept talking. "Things have moved fast with us," he said. "We both know it. So, we decided to slow down, take our time from here on out."

"And yet my daughter has a ring on her finger," her father, Harry, said. He hadn't introduced himself, but Kate had given

Jaime a rundown on all the important details—like names, like her being the oldest, like her dad recently retiring and taking up woodworking and having been given a workshop in the back yard by her mom for his birthday, complete with every tool under the sun.

Which meant there were plenty of sharp instruments in the vicinity.

Jaime held back a shudder and answered truthfully. "When you find someone worth holding on to, you don't let them go."

Silence, but he got the feeling that Kate's father approved.

Of that one thing he said, at least.

"And you didn't think you should meet us first? Didn't think you should ask permission before proposing?"

This question, or rather *questions*, came from Kate's brother, Jake.

He met the hostile blue eyes. "I think Kate is smart and capable enough to make the decision of who she wants to marry," he said, and it wasn't a line. Jaime believed it. He wouldn't have asked for permission from her dad to marry Kate. She was a strong, adult woman who could decide for herself. And *if* something like that was important to her—which he highly doubted based on the whole fake engagement thing —*maybe* then he would have given Harry a heads up that the proposal was coming. But he still wouldn't have asked permission. "As for meeting you guys, I did want to and am happy we finally got here. Between our work schedules—Kate's been working extremely hard, and I recently took over full time at my vet practice—along with wanting to keep this one thing for ourselves for just a little while—I come from a large family, too— time just got away from us."

"Sounds selfish," Jake said.

He shrugged. "Maybe, but I don't think it's selfish to spend time building a strong foundation with the woman who you're going to spend the rest of your life with."

The noise on the TV rose then, the crowd screaming as someone from the Gold scored, but Jaime didn't look away from Kate's brother.

Their gazes clashed—suspicion, irritation, frustration in Jake's, but Jaime held firm. If this fake engagement was going to turn into something more, then this was something he would need to overcome.

"How'd you know that sunflowers are Mary's favorite?" Harry asked, drawing Jaime's focus by referring to the bouquet he'd had stashed in the back seat and had given to Marabelle in the ten seconds he'd had before he'd been dispersed into the living room from hell.

"I didn't," he admitted. "But I know they're Kate's, and so I hoped that she would like them, too."

"And the whiskey?"

"My favorite," he said, "and my mom raised me to never come to a house empty-handed."

"Hmm." He turned his eyes back to the TV, and Jaime followed his gaze in time to see Liam Williamson make a move that even in slow motion was fast enough that he had to concentrate to see it.

He whistled. "Damn, he's good."

A beat, the tension hanging in the room for one more long moment then Harry chuckled and shook his head. "He's something else, that's for sure. Didn't think he'd be here for long, but he's certainly carved a niche out for himself here."

"Yeah," he said, "it was smart of them to put him with Coop and Blue. Their line has been almost unstoppable this season."

Feeling Jake's gaze on him, Jaime turned to face Kate's brother.

"You watch other sports?" Jake asked.

Jaime shrugged. "A little basketball and football, but I prefer hockey."

A glimmer of approval on the other man's face before he turned back to the game. "What do you think of Plantain this season?"

"Still recovering from that shoulder injury, but I'll bet she'll be back up to full strength before the playoffs," he said.

More quiet, but this silence—punctuated by the noise of the game playing in the background—wasn't homicidal, having him contemplating those power tools, or tense, two sets of eyes glaring. Instead, it had that glimmer of approval transforming into something more.

Not quite endorsement.

But he didn't think they'd be going to get the saw.

Good enough.

EIGHT

Kate

SHE WAS SWEATING as she arranged the bouquet of sunflowers Jaime had given to her mom—gorgeous, beautiful sunflowers that made her smile and want to steal them home for herself.

But the perspiration wasn't from the flowers.

It was because Jaime was confined in the other room with her brother and father, and based on the glares she'd seen when she'd walked by the space, it wasn't going to be a kumbaya moment.

They were going to rake the man who was doing her a favor, who was bailing her out, over the coals.

Fuck. She hadn't thought that through.

Frankly, she hadn't thought a *lot* of things through.

The ring. Her family—though her mom hadn't cared that she hadn't met Jaime because her oldest and perpetually single daughter was "engaged!!" (and yes, two exclamations were worthy of her mom's excitement). But she hadn't factored in the protectiveness of her brother and father, and how they'd always done the whole "you'd better take care of her, or you'll have me to answer to" thing.

That wasn't her favorite.

She could take care of herself.

But she appreciated that they loved her enough to worry, so while their protection had sometimes chaffed and often annoyed, she'd grown to accept it, oldest sibling who should be the one to be looking after the younger ones, or not.

Men being men.

Barf.

But also, it came from a good place. They wanted her safe and happy, and she couldn't deny that she'd also given Ann's then boyfriend now husband and Jake's wife the same narrow-eyed glare that her brother had been giving Jaime when she'd peeked in.

Ann was protective in a different way than she and Jake.

She'd be watching closely, cataloging, and be ready to step in the moment Jaime treated her the least bit wrong.

Her family might be annoying and nosy, but they also loved each other.

Plus, their nosiness meant that she got to be nosy right back, especially when it came to the dark circles under her sister's eyes.

"Did you talk to Dave?" she asked, forcing her gaze away from the living room and focusing on her sister. Who looked absolutely exhausted, and not just the typical post-baby exhaustion, but something more, something deeper.

Her sister sighed. "I tried. I don't know what's going on with him. He doesn't seem to hear me, and then when he does listen, he promises to do better, to help more."

"Then he doesn't?"

"No," Ann said. "He does, but then he disappears into his

own head again a-and—" She broke off, blue eyes swimming with tears.

"Come here," Kate said, wrapping an arm around her sister's waist and leading her from the room.

"The baby—"

"Mom's got her."

And their mom did. She was currently walking baby Lacy around the kitchen, telling her all about the colorful Christmas decorations. There was no way the two-month-old could understand her, let alone even see everything her mom pointed out, but Lacy was enraptured by her mom's musical voice anyway.

Kate smiled, thinking about all the times her mom had just talked to her, used her gentle, lyrical voice to talk her out of a tantrum, or off the edge of an argument with her best friend during her preteen years, or even helping her through a work problem.

She loved talking to her.

Minus the whole she-needed-to-be-in-a-relationship-or-her-womb-was-going-to-dry-up nonsense that had filled so many of their most recent conversations.

But now she had Jaime and hadn't heard about the doctor or so-and-so's cousin or anything about biological clocks.

It was glorious.

A lie.

She bit her lip, pushed the guilt away. So maybe it was a glorious lie, but she also had more to worry about in that moment than herself and the mess she'd made and the longing she felt growing with every minute she spent with Jaime.

For now, she needed to focus on her sister.

Keeping her arm around Ann, she snagged a blanket from the rack her mom kept by the back door and led them out onto the porch.

There were plenty of chairs around for them to sit in, but she didn't bother with that, instead walking Ann over to the top step, sitting her down, plunking down next to her, and then wrapping the blanket around them both. Picking up the thread of conversation, she said, "You say he disappears into his own head. How so?"

Ann's gaze was on the horizon, and it stayed that way for a long moment before she spoke. "It's like I'm talking to him and he's saying all of the right things, but he's not really there." She turned, eyes going to Kate's. "I feel so alone."

"Oh, sissy," Kate murmured, wrapping her other arm around her sister and hugging her tightly. "Have you told him that?"

"Yes." She paused, sniffed. "*No.* I mean, maybe not in those exact words?"

Since Dave had always made it clear that he thought Ann had hung the moon, Kate thought there might be more going on here than her sister could comprehend, especially given that Ann had spent the last months of her pregnancy on bed rest, had a difficult recovery after a challenging birth, and a colicky baby.

That was enough to throw anyone for a loop and most definitely enough to knock a couple off track.

"Why don't I watch Lacy next week, and you two can go out to dinner and really sit and talk it out?" she asked. "You both have been virtual zombies since Little Miss was born, and with him just going back to work, maybe he's having trouble adjusting?"

"What if she cries?"

Kate snorted. "She's a baby. She's *going* to cry."

"What if she's hungry?"

"I know you've been pumping and getting her used to a bottle once a day." She squeezed her sister's shoulder. "Let's plan the time around that."

"What if—?"

"You need to talk to him," she interrupted, starting to understand the problem. "And you need time and space to not be distracted to do so, and"—another squeeze—"you need to remember that I've been babysitting your ass since I was ten and you were three."

"I remember," Ann said dryly. "That's why I'm terrified of leaving my baby with you."

She made a face. "Hey!"

Ann smiled and the mischievous smirk along with the dry rejoinder made Kate relax. *That* was her sister—snark and teasing and an irresistible smile that made you beam at her in return. Not the exhausted female she'd been in her parents' kitchen.

And if Dave didn't get his shit together at this dinner, then Kate knew she'd take matters into her own hands.

If he thought her *mom* was pushy . . . well then he'd better watch out.

No one hurt her baby sister.

"Thanks, Katie," Ann said. "Can you watch her on Tuesday?"

She nodded, rested her head on Ann's shoulder. "Of course."

"You know," Ann murmured after they'd sat in silence for a few more minutes. "I almost understand why you didn't tell us about Jaime."

Oh, she did, did she?

But Kate shoved down the blip of guilt and asked, "Yeah?"

"Yes," Ann said. "I know it comes from a place of love, but Mom is a *lot*."

"You're just recognizing that?" Kate teased. "But you're right. She's amazing and has always been there for us, but she's also a whirlwind, and it can sometimes be tough to hold your ground." She paused. "Is that what you think is happening?"

"I don't know." Ann made a face. "Maybe? Okay"—a sigh —"yes. At least, I don't think it's helping. I mean, at first, I was so relieved to have her with me every day. But now . . . I think I need a little space. It's like between the wedding and then setting up our house and then Lacy . . . maybe part of what's going on with Dave and me is that we haven't had the space to settle into our own skin, you know?"

"I could see that," Kate murmured. "You two did move pretty fast with everything and then decided to throw a baby into the mix."

"Yeah." A sigh. "Damn."

"What?"

"I think I just gave myself two people to talk to, huh?" Her nose wrinkled. "I need to have heart-to-hearts with Mom and with Dave."

"Mom will take it okay," Kate said. "You know that. She's good at accepting boundaries once they're in place."

Blue eyes on hers. "And Dave?"

"Well, he's your husband," Kate said lightly, "and he loves you. I think you two can figure it out."

"I hope so."

Quiet fell between them. "You remember when Mom showed up at my dorm with homemade casseroles for the entire floor?"

Ann froze then burst out laughing. "Are you comparing my marriage to your tricky roommate situation?"

"Seemed apropos." She shrugged.

"I seem to remember that the boy you liked, who lived down the hall, suddenly asked you out after that."

"Yes, he did."

They'd actually gone on quite a few dates. They'd seen each

for months, long enough for her to feel comfortable with him, for her to fall in love. First love, freshman-in-college love, *stupid* love. Because she'd given him her virginity then had overheard him with his friends laughing about how bad she was in bed.

See? Assholes?

Her superpower.

Thankfully, she had been comfortable enough with herself to understand that it had been him—and his inability to last more than three thrusts, not to mention his lack in being able to please his partner—more than something she'd done.

So, she'd taken one of those casseroles her mom had left and dumped it in his lap.

And then she'd gone out with one of his roommates, who'd been much better in the sack and who'd taught her that she *could* have an orgasm during sex, so long as she was with someone who actually paid attention and had the patience to learn what she enjoyed.

So, asshole had met learning experience.

Thus, the path of her life had been laid.

Ha.

"Come on," she said, pushing to her feet and folding the blanket. "I don't know about you, but I'm starving."

She wasn't really. Not after the pastry and salad Jaime had bought her.

But she needed to do something that wasn't sitting on the back steps thinking about one of her asshole exes and then wondering if and when Jaime would become one of them.

Because as much as she liked him, felt a draw, enjoyed how sweet he was being, she also knew that at some point, the other shoe would fall.

And she didn't want to think about that.

Tucking the blanket under one arm, she extended her other toward her sister, giving her a hand up.

"What if it's because I haven't lost the baby weight? My body isn't the same and—"

A blip of fury flew through Kate.

"Then I'm cutting off his balls and feeding them to him," she growled. "You had a baby two months ago, sissy. If that's his problem, then I will cheerfully make him a eunuch and—"

"It's not."

Kate glanced up, saw that Dave was standing on the porch. She'd missed him opening the back door, missed him stepping out, but what she didn't miss was the fatigue and dark circles beneath his eyes.

And the concern in the pale brown depths.

Concern that made the fury slip away. Especially when he walked over to Ann and took her into his arms with barely a look at Kate.

As it should be.

"What the hell are you thinking, baby? I love you," he said, tone fierce. "Just the way you are. You're the most beautiful woman I have ever laid eyes on."

"I don't know what I'm thinking," Ann said. "I just feel so alone and . . ."

Heart squeezing, but glad that this conversation was taking place, even though it wasn't exactly how she and Ann had planned it out, Kate slipped through the back door, closed it, and hung up the blanket.

Then she walked down the hall, intending to help her mom with dinner.

Instead, when she strode into the kitchen and saw what was happening inside, every cell went to rigid attention, her breath caught, and her feet slid to a stop.

Because Jaime was in the kitchen.

Holding Lacy.

Swaying side to side as he rocked her gently, his big hand

cradled over the back her head, his palm on her back, rubbing circles.

She'd felt those circles, had that palm on her back.

Which was why this time it wasn't just her ovaries that exploded, but her heart as well.

NINE

Jaime

"YOU'RE GOOD WITH HER," Kate's mom said as she bustled around the kitchen.

"I'm the oldest of four," he told her, patting little Lacy's back when she began fussing again. "I did my fair share of babysitting."

Marabelle crossed by him, pulling out a carton of herbs from the fridge and pausing to pat his cheek. "You're a good boy."

"I don't know about that," he said, "but I do my best."

She smiled and shook her head but didn't argue with him.

"Can I do anything to help?"

"Besides hold the baby?" She slanted a look over at him. "No, honey, you just keep working your Lacy magic. I swear, she hasn't been this content since she was born."

He lifted Lacy up, smiling at the adorable little munchkin. Chubby cheeks, big eyes, a rosebud mouth, she was a beautiful baby. "Have you been giving your parents the run around?" Her face screwed up, and he wasn't sure if it was his question or because he'd dared switched positions. Quickly, he put her back against his shoulder, began rubbing circles on her back. Glancing up, he met Marabelle's amused eyes. "I guess that answers my question."

She laughed then turned her focus back to the sauce she was stirring.

"Where are your parents now?" she asked as he kept walking and rocking, gaze periodically going to the hall. He'd been able to catch a glimpse of Kate's bright red hair through the glass door on the back of the house. She and her sister had appeared to be in serious conversation.

So serious, in fact, that Dave, her sister's husband, had taken one glance at the sisters, wrapped in a blanket with their arms around each other, and had hustled down the hall, with hardly a look at the strange man who held his daughter.

"They're in Utah," he answered. "Most of my siblings are there, too. I came out for vet school at Davis, fell in love with the Bay Area, and never went home." Lacy cooed, drooling against his shoulder, and he smiled down at the tiny infant. Feisty, but also needing lots of love and care.

Kind of like her aunt.

But the good thing was that Jaime had plenty of love and care to give.

"Well, for my Katie's sake, I'm glad you stayed—oh, hi, honey. Everything okay with your sister?"

Jaime turned, saw that Kate had come back inside.

Her expression was soft, a swathe of pink across her cheeks, but it was her eyes that struck in him right in the heart.

Longing.

He was holding a baby, and she had longing in her eyes.

Their stares locked, held, and suddenly he was in the future.

In the same kitchen, with the same women, but holding a child that belonged to him, to them.

Lacy squawked, breaking the moment, knocking the vision from his mind even as he shifted her. But this time no amount of rocking or circles would calm her.

Kate moved over to a brightly printed diaper bag. "I'll just see if there's a bottle in here."

"It's in the fridge, honey," her mom said. "Bottle warmer is on the counter and set to go."

Kate nodded. "Got it."

Thirty seconds later, she'd retrieved the bottle, had it in and out of the warmer, and was testing the milk's temperature. "Gosh," she murmured, coming toward him. "I haven't done this since my babysitting days."

He grinned. "Me neither. None of my siblings have kids yet, much to my mom's chagrin." He bounced Lacy gently. "Though, as far as babysitting goes, I guess that's not *entirely* true—I spent a few days last spring bottle-feeding a litter of kittens." A shrug. "I guess that's a form of babysitting."

"Please, tell me you're kidding me," she said.

"No," he said. "Is this going to bring about more of your animal obsession?"

"They're *kittens*."

Jake came into the kitchen, headed for the fridge. "That's a yes, in case you were wondering."

"Kittens," Kate repeated, eyes bright. Then she smiled, that big grin that he felt like an actual caress across his skin, the one that made his heart swell and feel more than it had in years, and screwed the cap on the bottle, handing it to him. "Unless, you need a break?" she asked as he accepted it.

"I'm good," he said. "This involves significantly less of a need for octopus arms."

She laughed, Marabelle's chuckle following. "How many kittens were there?"

"Eight." A beat. "And they all wanted to eat at once."

"Naturally." Eyes dancing as she tapped a finger tapped against her bottom lip. "So, a true need for octopus arms."

He started giving Lacy the bottle, glad when she stopped fussing and began chugging the milk down like a champ. "Yup." A sly look. "Or an assistant with an obsession with all things furry. Know anyone who might be interested if the opportunity presents itself?"

She kissed his cheek. "No wedding unless you pick me."

Jaime turned his head, whispered in her ear. "Sold."

She blinked, lips parting, but then Jake laughed and punched his sister on the shoulder. "You might need to get a bigger yard, sis. If Jaime is in close proximity to animals at regular intervals, I think you're going to run out of space in that little garden of yours."

Kate swallowed, her gaze hot, but when she spoke, her tone was light. "He takes care of a rooster named Barry, who walks on a leash." As if that was the only evidence she needed to win any argument.

Jake glanced over at him, smirked. "I stand by my statement. You need a bigger yard."

Jaime smiled. "If Kate wants a rooster, she can have a rooster."

Marabelle beamed.

Jake sighed. "Dude, you've got to set the expectations low. You can't give them *everything* they want, or you'll never have negotiating power."

"I'm telling Steph you said that."

A narrowed look. "You wouldn't."

Kate danced away. "Why wouldn't I? It's my womanly duty to inform her of the underhanded tactics her husband uses."

"Plus," Marabelle said, "all she has to do is blink those pretty blue eyes and—"

A female voice intruded. "Are we talking about *my* pretty blue eyes?"

Jaime turned, saw a petite brunette had strode in, a laptop bag on her shoulder. She wore a black business suit and a tired expression. And for all his talk of negotiating power, Jake immediately crossed over to her and took her bag, cupping the side of her neck.

"Hi, baby," he murmured, kissing her lightly. "Work go okay?"

She nodded. "Fine. Now what's this about my eyes?"

"Jake said—"

Jake picked up a dish towel and chucked it at Kate, the floral-patterned cotton landing on her face with a quiet *swoosh*.

"Hey!" she exclaimed, yanking it off. "You—"

"Dinner time!" Marabelle called, interrupting the argument before it could really get going, in one of those quintessential Mom ways that told him all he needed to know about her parenting style.

She'd been there, been involved.

As thus, the kids—or well, adults—stopped arguing and got into gear, grabbing plates and napkins, side dishes, and a platter from the counter and carrying them into the dining room.

Ann appeared at his elbow, eyes slightly reddened, but a determined expression on her face, and he gently transferred Lacy into her arms. "She took the bottle?" she asked, surprise flitting across her face.

"Like a champ," he murmured.

She glanced up at her husband, and they shared a look that said more than words. Then he nodded and glanced over at Jaime. "Hi," he said. "Dave. Nice to meet you."

"You, too," Jaime said and nodded at Lacy. "She's adorable."

Ann smiled and ran a finger down her daughter's nose. "Thanks for feeding her."

"It was my pleasure," he said. "Babies are exhausting, and I figured you two could use a break. Thankfully, Kate got me set up with the bottle."

Kate came up to him, getting close, and instinct had him wrapping his arm around her, tugging her to his side. "Jaime bottle-fed kittens last spring," she said then added in a stage-whispered, "and he promised me a rooster."

Two pairs of wide eyes on him and all he could do was chuckle.

"I don't know if it was quite a promise," he prevaricated.

"Told you," Jake said with a sigh. "You've lost that negotiating power and—"

This time, Steph was the one who tossed the dish towel. And with perfect accuracy, he might add. It landed across Jake's face, muffling anything further he might have said, and then as though it were something she'd done a hundred times before, she turned to Jaime, stuck her hand out, and said, "Hi, I'm Steph. Welcome to the crazy."

He grinned as he shook it. "Jaime. And I have to say, the crazy is more than welcome."

Marabelle snagged his elbow, lacing her arm through his. "I'm glad you say that because—"

"Mom," Kate said.

"I was wondering—"

"*Mom,*" Kate repeated.

"—if you'd like to see Kate's baby pictures," Marabelle finished, not acknowledging Kate's groan, continuing to talk as though her daughter hadn't said a word. "I have this great shot of her naked in the tub and—"

"Mom!"

She winked, released his arm, and began shepherding them into the dining room.

"I'm kidding about the naked tub picture," Marabelle added.

Kate sighed, and he stifled a smile.

"Because I have a naked spaghetti picture that's so much better."

Jaime couldn't help it. He burst out laughing. Kate smacked him, grabbed his arm, dragging him to a halt in the hall, and gasping in outrage.

"Don't you dare laugh!"

Then there was another thing he couldn't help, and that was turning and brushing his fingers over Kate's cheek, bending down to drop a kiss to her lips that was semi-chaste. Chaste because there was no tongue, but semi because it probably went on longer than it should have, considering they were in her parents' house and he'd met them all of an hour before.

But she was like a drug.

One touch, and he wanted more. One kiss, and he wanted to run his lips over every inch of her body.

One night, and he wanted an eternity.

The sound of a throat clearing had Jaime slowing the kiss. He dropped his forehead against hers, his breath coming in short bursts and whispered, "Sorry."

Warm whiskey eyes on his. "For what?"

"That wasn't exactly what I planned."

A heated smile. "Feel free to kiss me like that any time you want."

He lifted his head, brushed back some of the red silken tresses that had crept forward to tangle on her cheek. "I'm going to take you up on that."

Lacing his fingers with hers, he stepped away, saw that her dad was studying them closely, his expression fierce, though it gentled when it shifted over to his daughter.

"Come on, Katie girl," he murmured. "Let's eat before it gets cold."

Those eyes, so like Kate's, flicked to him, and instead of the rebuke Jaime had expected to see, Harry nodded at him approvingly.

Kate squeezed his hand, whispered, "Ready for more of my family?"

He nodded, having more fun than he'd had in ages. "Yeah, Red, bring it on."

They followed Harry into the dining room, and he was hardly one step over the threshold when Ann said, "Jaime?"

He glanced her way, noted the mischief on her face, and braced himself.

And found out approximately half a second later that it had been the wisest course of action because her next question was, "What does Kate have to do to get you to buy her a real diamond?"

TEN

Kate

IT HAD BEEN the best night ever.

Jaime reached across her after she'd sat down in the passenger's seat and buckled her seat belt. She didn't protest the action, nor the kiss he brushed to her forehead, too exhausted after the workday, after the emotional conversation with Ann, after the dinner filled with laughing and teasing and so much love, after . . . spending the evening living a lie that didn't actually feel like a lie.

She wanted it to be real.

So fucking much.

"You okay?" he murmured.

Kate nodded, forced a smile. "Just tired."

Pale brown eyes holding hers. "Sure?"

She nodded again, heart thumping when he ran his thumb over her bottom lip. But then he was stepping back, hand going to the door. "Well, then, let's get you home."

"I—"

The door closed, cutting off her sentence.

Which was just as well because she was probably going to say something stupid like, "I don't want to go home yet."

But she *needed* to go home.

She needed to remind herself that Jaime wasn't hers, not really. He wasn't *her* man, the one whose gaze had connected with hers over Lacy's head, the longing in his eyes no doubt matching hers. He wasn't her man who'd charmed her mom and sister, who'd calmed the overprotectiveness of her brother and father.

He wasn't even her man who'd fallen for her over a ketchup bottle.

But he *was* the man who'd thought to bring her a ring, who'd bought her lunch and looked at her with open desire, who laughed and smiled freely, who touched her gently and frequently, who buckled her seat belt and showed up at a restaurant after a long and complicated procedure because he was worried that she hadn't gotten his message.

He was a good man.

And that probably should have been enough to slap her fantasy-addled mind into reality.

Because good men didn't want her.

Her door opened again, and suddenly Jaime was there, his mouth inches away from hers, hot breath on her lips, hands holding her face.

"Don't be sad, Red," he murmured.

Embarrassed, she started to turn away, not liking that he could read her so easily, abruptly hating that he'd been able to insert himself into her life so effortlessly. That was dangerous because she was going to miss him when he was gone.

"I'm fine," she said, deliberately not meeting his eyes, not when he saw so much.

His stare she was avoiding felt heavy on her face, but she still didn't turn to meet it, didn't offer up any more words, and after a moment, Jaime brushed his thumb over her cheek. "I like you, Kate," he said. "A lot. Your family, too. And that has not one fucking bit to do with the fact that the ring you're wearing isn't real."

Her lungs had frozen at the first statement.

By the time he'd made it to the end of his words and had dropped his hands, stepping back and closing the door for a second time, they burned from an utter lack of oxygen.

He paused as he rounded the hood, eyes locking onto hers, and she found that she could breathe again. Sucking in much-needed oxygen, she watched him continue on, heard the slight *pop* from his door opening, felt the car move as he sat down and buckled in, heard the rumble of the engine as he pressed the button to start the ignition.

What she *didn't* hear?

More words.

The man, the good man, was giving her time to process.

He pulled out of the driveway, the path slightly more difficult to maneuver as Ann and Dave had ridden home together, leaving Dave's car parked behind them and bundling a sleeping Lacy into the back seat of Ann's SUV.

Whatever was going on with them had been somewhat tempered by the conversation on the back porch. Ann's eyes were slightly reddened from tears, Dave's lined in exhaustion, but they'd held hands throughout dinner, and Kate had approved of the fact that Dave hadn't left her sister's side.

Ann didn't have Kate's asshole superpower.

It needed to stay that way.

Only one McLeod should have that particular ability, and it definitely shouldn't be her sweet, lovely sister.

Nope, the burden alone was Kate's.

You know what they say, she thought snarkily, *with great power comes great responsibility.*

Ha.

"My ex messed me up."

She had let her eyes slide closed, her brain sinking in a soft haze, full of reality, but also full of pleasure. Because she'd seen joy in her mom's face, approval in her dad's. Because Jaime fit.

His words, however, had her eyes flying open, had her shifting in her seat to look at him.

So fucking handsome.

A strong jaw, a straight nose, plump, kissable lips, short —*frown*—hair.

And gorgeous.

As though her brain had conjured every action star fantasy in her brain and had mashed them all together into her living, breathing dream man.

Who was nice. Who was sweet.

Who was *sharing*.

"What happened?" she asked softly. "What did she do?"

His fingers shifting on the steering wheel, gripping tightly as he maneuvered the car around a turn. "It's been long enough that I know that it's what we *both* did," he said, the half of his mouth she could see curved up into a smile. "She was really good at getting under my skin and could be mean as a snake, but I was also really good at letting her manipulate me and didn't cut ties and run at those first red flags." His gaze shifted to hers then back to the road. "And those first red flags were plentiful."

"I'm sorry," she said, reaching over and squeezing his leg, before adding lightly, "What's her name so I can hate her properly?"

He chuckled. "See?"

Her brows drew together. "See what?"

"You're nothing like her," he said. "I knew that from two minutes into dinner, knew that even though I wanted to paint you with the same brushstrokes—because even though I

wanted to know you better, it was safer for my heart if I didn't
—that I couldn't." He took one hand off the wheel, covered hers
where it was resting on her thigh. "You're lovely and sweet and
funny, and have that quintessential human feeling called
empathy."

Wow.

"Was she that bad?"

Another glance. "Take what you're imagining and make it a
hundred times worse." His fingers tightened on the steering
wheel again. "But I still stayed for too long. So fucking stupid."

"No," she whispered. "That's called human."

"Po-tay-to, po-tah-to," he muttered.

She giggled then sobered. "I am sorry, you know? I've dated
some men who—" She shuddered.

"What are their names, so I can hate them properly?"

Her heart fluttered.

"Scratch that, what are their names, so I can kill them
properly?"

She touched his cheek. "You're sweet."

He turned his head, pressed a kiss to her palm. "You're used
to giving a lot of yourself, aren't you?"

"What do you mean?"

"Your heart is generous," he said. "You see someone hurting
and you jump in, you make it better."

Kate shrugged. "I have a weak spot for people, I guess. I like
to see them happy."

Silence.

"But who makes sure *you're* happy?" he asked. "If you only
give of yourself and never take, who cares for you, Red?"

Her breath caught, that question hitting way too close to the
vulnerable center of her. Giving meant she controlled the inter-
actions, controlled how much of herself she gave, and meant she
could always keep a piece back.

She'd learned long ago she always needed to keep a piece of herself protected and safe.

Because sometimes it was only that single piece that remained, that single piece she had to hold tightly on to as she rebuilt herself brick by brick.

But she couldn't tell him that.

She could barely accept it herself, preferred to pretend everything was light and easy.

"Empathy is an important life skill," she said, her tone teasing as she added, "So your ex had an inhuman lack of it?"

They slid to a stop at a signal, and Jaime turned his gaze on hers.

Then studied her for a long moment.

Panic bubbled up because, damn, he wasn't going to let her go.

"Alien, maybe," he muttered. "Because I've seen more empathy in animals than my ex had."

Kate squeezed his leg again. "Her name, please, good sir," she said, relieved he hadn't pushed enough to joke. "Hate will be commencing shortly."

He snorted. "Lori."

"Ugh," she muttered. "I knew a Lori in high school. She was the worst sort of bully."

He laughed. "Must be the name."

"Maybe." She bit her lip, a tendril of guilt weaving through her. She actually had a Lori on her design team, and design-team-Lori was really lovely.

"That." Fingers lifting from her hand, drifting over her cheek. "That's how I knew you weren't like Lori." A chuckle. "You were feeling guilty for lumping the whole of the Lori populace into one group, weren't you?"

"I work with a nice Lori and—"

He burst out laughing. "Fuck, but I like you, Kate."

Her heart somehow managed to swell with pleasure and also curl in on itself protectively. God, she liked him, too. But—

"Don't say that," she murmured. "You *can't*. You can't like me, can't make me like you because then when it's over, when you're done with me, it'll hurt too much." She pulled her hand back, sat up straight in her own seat. "I can't like you, not like that, not enough to want a future."

Silence.

Long, drawn-out silence.

Then the car shuddered to a stop on the shoulder, and he turned to face her. "Why can't you want a future, Kate?"

"Why do you care?" she snapped. "This is a fake relationship. It doesn't mean *anything*."

A deadly calm. "Doesn't it?"

"No!" She tossed her hands up. "We've gone on one date—"

"Two."

Frowning, she stopped. "What?"

"Technically tonight was the second."

That threw her for a loop, and she froze. "Okay," she said, unfreezing after a couple of seconds. "So, two dates. That doesn't mean anything."

"Doesn't it?"

She crossed her arms, sighed heavily. "You already asked that."

"And you're sticking with the answer *no?*" More calm, his voice so smooth, so even, but below the surface she could sense a fury boiling, and she knew, *just knew*, that the asshole was going to rear its head.

Still, she might like this man too much, but she wasn't a fucking weakling. She held his gaze, straightened her spine, and braced herself for the impact that was sure to be lobbed her way.

And stayed braced.

And stayed a little longer.

Then longer still, waiting, knowing he was going to blow up at her.

Eventually, he shifted in his seat, and she jumped, not wanting to, knowing it gave away too much, revealed how brittle and on edge she was.

But she hadn't been able to help it.

Jaime ran the back of his fingers over her throat, making her shiver, and his words when he spoke after that long moment of silence were gentle, were light. "Then I guess I'll just have to prove it to you."

She swallowed hard, missing his hand when he brought it back to the steering wheel. "Prove what?"

Eyes locked onto hers for a searing moment. "That you mean something."

Those words, said in that gentle, light tone, wafted across the console to her ears, but when her brain processed them, their impact might as well have been a bullet to her gut.

They seared into her, branded themselves on her heart.

He leaned over and slanted his mouth against hers.

It was a quick, hot touch of his lips to hers . . . and it still scorched her down to the bone.

"You mean something to me, Kate," he murmured before pulling back onto the road and driving her home, as though he hadn't just rocked her to the core.

ELEVEN

Jaime

HE WOKE up the next morning to a text that made his heart—the one that was thinking he'd pushed Kate too hard the night before—swell with hope.

The truth was that he was all in for her, and seeing her stare at him, wariness written in the lines of her pretty face, made him feel like shit. He got that it was less to do with him and more to do with her past, but part of him was worried that he wouldn't be able to break through the barrier she'd placed between them.

Maybe not a deliberate barrier. Perhaps she'd been hurt often enough that the barrier was a permanent fixture.

"Patience," he murmured to himself, rolling onto his back and sitting up.

Because . . . the text.

Sent at two in the morning, even though she'd been exhausted on the drive home, even after he'd deliberately turned the conversation to something light—movies and favorite restaurants.

The dark circles had seemed to get darker as he'd driven.

Dark enough that he'd eventually stopped talking, stopped trying to think of easy conversational topics that wouldn't put her on the defensive, and he'd thought there was a real possibility that she might fall asleep on the drive.

She hadn't.

In fact, *he'd* fallen. Fallen further, deeper, more entrenched in that woman.

Because then she'd asked about his family—had laughed when he'd described the group text chain he had with his siblings and parents, and how his younger brother, Brad, had left his phone on a table at a restaurant recently and they'd all been treated to a series of emoji-filled texts that took up the entire screen of his cell, courtesy of a rambunctious toddler from the next booth over.

"You need to take lessons from him on emoji-etiquette."

"From the toddler?"

She nodded.

He laughed. "Is this a lesson of more is better?"

A snort. "I take it back." She smiled at him, the barrier still there, but hidden beneath brown eyes sparkling with amusement. "Stick with your book."

Fun. Teasing. Sweet. Smile that fucking took his breath

Actually listening to him when he talked. Touching him when she forgot she was supposed to be keeping her distance—a squeeze on his leg, a brush of fingers on his arm, his jaw.

And now she'd sent him a text in the middle of the night.

I'm sorry about Lori. You deserve someone who sees the wonderful man you are inside.

Absently, he rubbed a hand over his chest, his heart aching. Sweet. See?

But also, completely blind to the fact that she was wonderful on the inside as well, blind to the notion that a man wanted to wrap himself in the warmth of her, to capture the light in her soul and hold it captive.

Because someone had made her believe she wasn't worthy of that.

Which circled back to his notion of Jaime being all in for this woman.

First, he wanted to get her some fucking glasses so that when she looked at herself in the mirror, she saw how wonderful she was. Second, he wanted to hunt down the asshole or assholes that made her believe differently.

But in reality, he couldn't do either of those things until he managed to get through her shields.

Well, luckily, he wasn't an idiot.

He recognized a good thing when he saw it, knew that she was worth the effort to gain her trust.

Which was why he didn't text her back.

Instead, he got up and showered.

Instead, he went down to the Farmer's Market and picked up a bouquet of sunflowers, a half dozen pastries, and two coffees—a mocha for her, just black for him—then drove to her house, glad that they lived close enough that the early Saturday morning drive to her place made the drinks' temperature drop to drinkable rather than cold and unappetizing.

He parked in front of her house and felt the bottom drop out of his plan. Or hell, maybe it was the bottom dropping out of his world, him plummeting through the hole, falling and falling further.

He'd been thinking he would text, and if that didn't work, then he'd call her, and then if *that* didn't work, he'd go up to her front door and knock or ring the bell.

He'd even gone so far as to convince himself that she'd open the door and would be standing sleepily on the other side wearing fluffy pajamas, her hair askew, cozy sheep-shaped slippers on her feet.

Yes, he had an overactive imagination.

But even his overactive imagination had not imagined short-shorts and a hoodie. He hadn't been able to picture Kate bending over a flowerpot on her front porch, her luscious ass and long, *long* legs on display. He certainly wouldn't have been able to conjure up the unzipped hoodie, the thin and worn tank top beneath.

Thankfully, he was already parked at the curb. Otherwise, the gorgeous flowers she had lining the walkway that led up to her house might have ended up under his tires.

Straightening, she turned, that gorgeous ass disappearing. But he wasn't disappointed, not when he got to meet those beautiful eyes through the windshield.

He grabbed the sunflowers, the bag of pastries, and the coffees then popped open the driver's side door.

"Jaime?"

The soft question greeted him before he closed the door behind him, and the sound of his name on her tongue sent heat arrowing toward his cock.

But he wasn't here to be led around by his cock.

He was here with a plan to win over this smart, sweet, beautiful on the inside and out woman. To chip a hole through the concrete and make a place for himself in her heart.

So, he kept his tone even and walked over to her, handing her the flowers. "Morning, Red."

Her voice was husky. "Morning, Jaime." She bit at that bottom lip. "Thank you," she murmured. "They're beautiful."

"You're welcome." His eyes dipped down, lingered on all

that exposed skin. He was thanking whatever God had created short shorts when he let his gaze come back up, connect with hers. "Morning, my *sexy* Red."

Okay, so maybe not being led around by his cock by this woman was an impossible task, especially when all she had to do was breathe and he was hard.

Pink painted itself across her cheeks, and her lips parted as she inhaled a shaky breath. "What are you doing here?" she asked.

He held up the bag, the coffees. "Bringing you breakfast." A beat. "Though, I didn't expect to find you out of bed yet."

"Oh."

At the question in her eyes, he added. "You texted pretty late last night."

This time her cheeks didn't go pink. Rather, they paled, and her eyes shifted to the side. "Oh, yeah. I-I—" She stammered for a moment then murmured, "I hope I didn't wake you up."

"My cell is always on Do Not Disturb at night," he said. "I learned my lesson after getting way too many calls from the clinic when it wasn't my turn to be on call."

"Oh . . . good," she murmured.

"Is that your favorite word in the mornings?"

Red brows drew together. "What?"

"*Oh*," he said, setting the coffees down on the porch railing. "Is it your favorite word in the mornings?"

Those brows stayed drawn. "No."

"Okay." He shrugged, sat down on the top step. "So, you couldn't sleep last night?"

"I—well—"

He pulled out an apple turnover, offered it to her. "Hungry?"

She glanced down at her hands, and he saw they were

covered in dirt. Then she bit her lip again. Fuck, but he thought that was sexy as hell, even as he recognized it was because she was unsure.

Shoving the turnover back into the bag, he stood and set it alongside the coffees on the railing. Then he snagged her hand, drew her over to the hose spigot he'd spied on his walk up the house, and rinsed off her hands. The dirt disappeared, and he used the bottom of his shirt to dry her fingers, her palms.

Maybe not the most sanitary, but it had given him an excuse to touch her, to bring her close.

And now they could eat.

"Come on." He nudged her over to the porch and down onto the front step. Then he grabbed her coffee. "Mocha," he said and handed it to her.

Her brows lifted. "How'd—?"

"I pay attention." When those brows stayed lifted, he added, "I've seen you express your undying love for them on many an Insta post."

She smiled, shook her head. "Thank God I keep my profile private for everyone except for sexy vets."

Mock-glowering, he asked, "How *many* sexy vets?"

"Hmm." She tapped a finger to her chin. "That is an excellent question."

"Okay, *questionee*"—he plunked the bag of pastries on her lap—"the next question you must answer is which sweet treat do you want?"

Her mouth curved. "I think the question is what sweet treat do *you* want?"

And Jaime found he couldn't resist the invitation.

He leaned over and kissed her.

Soft lips parted immediately, and he slipped his tongue inside her mouth, tangled it against hers. She tasted of mint and coffee, making his senses come alive, heat spreading out over his skin. Never had a simple kiss aroused him more, but then again, this woman was *more*.

She had the potential to be everything.

So, when she set the coffee and the bag aside then wrapped her arms around his neck and leaned back, tried to pull him on top of her, Jaime forced himself to stop.

To gentle the kiss, coaxing her down from the edge, pulling them back millimeter by millimeter until their lips separated. He stayed close, fingers in her ponytail, rapid breaths mixing. "You are so fucking beautiful."

A sharp inhale, her eyes closing for a heartbeat.

Hope. Fear. Pain. Desire. They swirled in those whiskey-colored depths, and he wanted to magnify the first and last, needed to make the middle two disappear.

He released her hair, had to physically force himself to straighten up, to not kiss that slightly swollen mouth and fill her with so much need and pleasure that she forgot all about the fear of the future, the pain of the past. She would be enveloped in desire, smothered in it, coating every inch as he gave her orgasm after orgasm.

And maybe that was ego talking, but also . . . he didn't think it was *all* ego.

They had chemistry, and it was combustible. Dry tinder in the forest, just needing the slightest spark in order to burst into flames.

Need coiled in his gut, fingers clenching, wanting to explore more.

Patience, remember?

Stifling a sigh, he nodded inwardly. That was the plan. Patience and winning her over.

He picked up the bag. "Breakfast."

Kate clasped a hand to her chest and the sight of her parted lips, breaths coming in rapid inhalations and exhalations had Jaime locking his spine, clenching one hand into such a tight fist that his bones ached.

"Breakfast," he said again, starting to hand her the bag.

She wrapped her fingers around his, halted the bag in mid-air. "What if I said I wasn't interested in breakfast?" she asked quietly. "What if I said that I wanted to kiss you again instead?"

His dick twitched. His fingers tightened on the brown paper, making it crinkle loudly in the quiet of the morning. His jaw clenched.

She stretched up, kissed the ticking muscle. "So tense."

"Such a tease," he murmured, covered her hand with his free one. "Wearing those sexy shorts." He dropped his palm to her bare thigh, slid it up an inch, fingers tracing light circles when her breath caught. "Kissing me until I can't think, can't remember all the reasons I'd been promising myself to give you romance."

Her mouth curved. Her eyes went soft. "Were there a lot of reasons?"

"I made a list."

She giggled, the tinkling sound sliding over his skin, helping him wrench himself back under control.

Then she bit her lip again, her eyes taking on a slightly guilty expression.

"What?" he rasped out.

That gorgeous mouth parting, the shuddering exhale drifting over his skin. "I made a list, too," she said, all soft. And close. She was close enough that the floral smell of her shampoo drifted over him, mixed with the damp earth scent of the garden, the humid perfume of the morning air.

His hand clenched on her thigh, and she jumped.

"Sorry," he murmured, relaxing his hold, not wanting to ever hurt her.

"No." She placed her palm over his, squeezed lightly. "It felt good."

More heat. More dick twitching. More of his control fading. More of his plan disappearing into so much smoke.

Jaime traced patterns on her silken skin, feeling goose bumps rise from the contact.

"Aren't you going to ask about my list?" she eventually asked.

Her pupils were dilated, that tempting fucking mouth too close, but there was also mischief in her gaze, warming the brown of her irises, and he wanted her to feel comfortable enough to tease, to play, even if it meant tormenting him with all her sexy skin and lip-biting and a list he thought was going to put his control to the test.

"Yes."

Her brows rose expectantly.

He grinned. "What's on your list, Red?"

Pink on her cheeks, even though she was the one who'd pressed the issue, but the mischief was also still there as she glanced up at him with dancing eyes and put it right out there. "It's a list of all the places I've imagined you kissing me."

There was no tempering his reaction, no holding on to his control.

Her soft mix of shy and not had obliterated any hope he had of pulling back.

He dropped the much-abused bag, knew the pastries inside were probably already reduced to crumbs and not giving one damn. Her thigh that was under his palm tightened, and he groaned, continued massaging the strong muscle that was covered in silk. His other hand went to her cheek, thumb shifting to rub against her bottom lip.

"Did you imagine me kissing you here?" he asked, voice filled with gravel.

She nodded, eyes hot, huskiness invading her words. "Yes."

He dipped his head and slanted his lips across hers, taking her mouth in a kiss that was pure desire, fanning the flames of his need until he was almost surprised to not find himself reduced to ash.

Only when he felt like his lungs would explode did he release Kate's mouth.

Her chest rose and fell in rapid succession, her fingers clenching the fabric of his T-shirt. Her body so close and so fucking tempting.

He ran his knuckles along the column of her throat. "What about here?"

She nodded.

Jaime bent and pressed his lips to the side of her neck, nipping lightly then soothing the slight sting with his tongue.

She gasped, threaded her fingers into his hair and tugged. "*Oh!*"

"Fuck, I love the way you say that," he murmured, stealing a quick hard kiss from her mouth just because he could, but also because he couldn't resist those lips. He stroked a finger lower, dipped it into the front of her tank top. "What about here?"

"No." She grabbed his hand, brought it to her breast. "I imagined you kissing me here."

The edges of his vision went hazy.

"Kate—"

Her fingers twitched, which meant that *his* fingers twitched, and holy hell the feel of her beneath his hand, soft and squeezable and damned near overfilling his hold was. So. Freaking. Glorious.

"Will you?" she murmured, shifting slightly, and he felt the hard bud of her nipple brush against his palm. "Will you kiss me here, Jaime?"

Fuck the pastries.

Fuck the coffee.

Fuck the plan.

He swept her up into his arms and carried her into the house.

TWELVE

Kate

THAT WAS PERHAPS the boldest request she had ever made.

But damn, had it paid off.

Because now she was in Jaime's arms, pressed against the chest she'd admired in so many of his pictures, held close as he stood and pushed through the front door of her house.

A moment of her weight shifting, but before she could do more than grip his shoulders a little tighter, the lock *clicked,* and she was pulled even closer.

She expected him to ask her where her bedroom was, to dump her down onto the mattress, to cover her body with his own and strip her naked. She expected him to take advantage of the opening she gave him, to take everything she had freely offered to him.

And that would have been fine.

Because it *had* been freely offered.

Because she wanted that, too.

Had dreamed about it, had fantasized and imagined and

hoped and prayed it would come about, and in this moment, she couldn't think of anything she wanted more.

But then he spun and pressed her to the door, pinning her against the hard wood.

His lips curved up at the corners. His eyes went hot.

And then he said, "Where else can I kiss you, Red?"

She wrapped her legs around his hips, lurched up so her mouth was a hairsbreadth from his. "*Everywhere.*"

Lips curving further. Fingers sliding into her hair, knocking the ponytail askew, his hips holding her in place against the wood, and his free hand slipping under the hem of her tank top, his palm scalding where it met her bare skin. "Yeah?"

Kate nodded. "Yeah."

He dropped to his knees so fast that she shrieked.

But he only stayed there for a moment, long enough to unhook her legs, to help her find her feet, and then he was rising up, and his lips were on hers.

Long and slow and deep, he kissed her as though she were the tastiest dessert on the planet, and he intended to savor every bite. His tongue licked across her lips, slipped inside, and caressed hers, coaxing her into a rhythm that made her thighs clench, her knees tremble.

And all the while, his hands were moving, combing through her unbound hair, stroking up and down her side, over her stomach in delicate circles. A gentle pattern with slightly roughened skin that threatened to melt her into a puddle of goo.

His hand slid up, stopping an inch beneath her bra, and her breasts swelled, her nipples hard little points that ached for his mouth.

"Jaime," she breathed.

"Red." He touched her cheek and crouched again, hunkering down in front of her. He was so much taller than her and when he went down to his knees for a second time, his mouth was positioned exactly where she wanted.

He leaned in, sucked the hard bud of her nipple into his mouth.

She still wore her tank top, her bra. Together they made up several layers of fabric. So, him touching her that way shouldn't have felt good, shouldn't have sent desire spiraling through her body like his touch was a live wire directly to her pussy. But this was Jaime.

And the fact that he held such a power over her wasn't scary.

Because she knew deep down in the depths of her soul that he wouldn't take advantage of that power, that he wouldn't hold it over her, that she would be safe with him.

Because she also knew that somehow, she held the same power over him.

Flick.

She jumped.

Glanced down to see he'd tugged open the button on her shorts.

Her breath caught at the sight of his hands just below her navel, broad fingers tugging the pull of her zipper down. He spread the fabric, denim worn so often over the years that it had grown soft, that it was thin and fraying.

"Unicorns."

He smiled, pressed his lips against the fabric of her underwear, bright purple and dotted with dancing unicorns.

It wasn't sexy or skimpy. But then again, she hadn't expected to have a man between her thighs that morning.

Her hands slid between them, self-consciousness bubbling up, wanting to cover up the ridiculous fabric, but then Jaime took her hands, pressed them, palms flat, against the door.

"I like it," he murmured, the words coming against her skin, hot and damp and making her need spiral up and out of control. She barely felt when he lifted one of her feet then the other, tugging off her shoes and chucking them aside because his lips were moving in time with his hands, sliding up, nudging her tank top out of his way. He gripped the arms of her hoodie and that too disappeared, then her shirt was tugged over her head. "Unicorns," he said, still speaking against her skin, still moving up, only this time he pushed her bra out of the way. "*You're* the unicorn, my beautiful, sweet Kate."

"I'm not—"

The sentence didn't get a chance to form because then his mouth closed over her nipple.

Her words devolved into a moan. Her hands went to his hair, gripped tight.

Thankfully, Jaime didn't stop. Instead, he continued drawing on her nipple, shifting so he could take the other between thumb and forefinger, rolling gently at first, then harder until she was moaning, her hips bucking, her pussy clenching because she needed . . . more.

She needed him.

As though she'd spoken aloud, he began sliding his hand down her side, insinuated it between them, between the fabric of her underwear and her shorts, and cupped her.

"No," she gasped, fingers still tight in his hair.

He growled, nipped the underside of her breast. "No," he agreed. "Skin."

"Yes," she moaned. "Please, Jaime."

One shove had her panties and shorts around her ankles, another abrupt movement had them tugged off her legs. One more had her thighs spread wide.

His eyes met hers, fire in those pale brown depths, and held for a long moment. Then he dropped his gaze, and she felt the slow slide of his heated stare drift down her neck, caress over her breasts, trace over her stomach, dip lower, and hold.

"So pretty and pink and glistening."

She choked but didn't have time to say anything because Jaime was already moving, shifting forward and lifting one of her legs so it was over his shoulder.

And then his mouth was on her.

Or rather, his tongue.

He traced it through her damp folds, sliding over her sensitive labia, until he pressed the flat part to her clit, firm and sure and making sparks flash behind her eyes. Not rushing, but moving slow and steady, his caresses designed to discover exactly what she liked and then using the knowledge ruthlessly.

She'd been turned on from the moment he opened his car door and she saw it was him. She'd been wet from the second his palm had touched her thigh. She'd been on razor's edge from the instant her nipple was drawn deep into his mouth.

So, it was no surprise that his tongue on her clit, its rhythm perfect, and his finger circling the entrance to her body before pushing slowly inside would catapult her over the edge in mere seconds.

She exploded, pleasure coating her skin from head to toe in wave after wave after wave of pure, unadulterated bliss.

Thus was the power of Jaime.

THIRTEEN

Jaime

SHE WAS asleep in his arms.

Which was so not his plan.

It was also so much better.

She'd come on his fingers, his tongue, crying out his name. He'd never thought he would be the type of guy who would crave a woman saying his name, but Jaime couldn't deny that hearing it roll off Kate's tongue was music to his ears.

Then again, anything she seemed to say was music to his ears.

To his soul.

Sappy.

But finding a good woman would do that to a man, especially one as beautiful and wonderful and lovely as Kate.

He'd carried her to the couch, had wrapped them both in a blanket, though he hadn't needed anything more than her naked body pressed to his in order to be warm, to be scorched through down to the bone.

Her eyes had stayed closed, and she'd cuddled close and . . . he'd lost another piece of himself.

Fingers sliding through her hair, gliding down her arm, taking full advantage of the fact that she was asleep, that she trusted him enough already to have let exhaustion and pleasure take her over while in his arms, to study her closely. She appeared unguarded, and just so damned young.

They were the same age, and when she was conscious, that similarity was obvious, made clear by the shadows present in her eyes, the tension in her frame.

But like this, expression gentled, sleep making the rosebud of her lips shape into a tiny O every time she exhaled, and Jaime thought that she could be much, much younger.

Maybe not in age but in spirit.

Smiling when he thought of what her response would be to that —she'd tease him and his poetry skills, of that he had no doubt—he stayed in place, stroking her hair, watching the sun get a little higher, the sky a bit brighter before she stirred, nuzzling at his throat, her breathing changing from to slow and steady to slightly faster.

Then she froze, ramrod stiff in his arms.

She was awake.

And naked.

Conscious that she might be feeling uncomfortable, he slipped out from beneath the blanket, careful to leave it covering her, then made his way into the hall.

Panties tangled with her shorts, both shoved in the corner.

Bra one way. Her tank top the other.

He gathered them all up and snagged her hoodie, which had somehow ended up on the coatrack, then headed back to her, setting them on the couch next to her.

She was staring out the front windows when he walked in, gaze on the lush greenery that was dotted with purple flowers, jumped when he placed the pile on the cushion beside her thigh.

Her eyes flew to his, a blush crept into her cheeks. "Jaime—"

He ran his knuckles over her cheek. "I'll go make some coffee."

"I—" Teeth digging into her bottom lip.

"Coffee first," he murmured, running his thumb lightly over her skin.

More hesitation then she nodded.

He went back into the hallway, moved to the opening he'd spied on his limited travels, and moved to the Keurig. Opening a couple of cabinets led him to a set of purple glasses lined up neatly next to a stack of purple plates.

Her favorite color is purple.

Remembering her quick recital from the other night had him smiling.

It seemed that her favorite extended to plates and cups. His eyes flicked to the right.

And coffee mugs, he realized, reaching past the tidy rows of purple drinkware to retrieve a pair of lilac ceramic cups, plunked them on the counter, and stuck a mocha pod in the coffee maker, then set the machine to run. Once it was working, he slipped out the front door and retrieved the bag of pastries, pleased to find out there were more than crumbs inside.

By the time he made his way back to the kitchen and was placing a slightly squished pumpkin muffin, an apple turnover with one end broken off, and a peppermint scone on the plate, Kate came in, fully dressed.

Now that was a disappointment.

The color was still high in her cheeks, but her eyes when they met his were soft. "Sorry, I fell asleep on you," she murmured. "I . . . um . . . didn't get much rest last night."

He set down the bag, crossed over to her.

"My fault," he said, tracing a hand down her arm, relieved when she didn't back away, when she let him lace his fingers through hers and hold tight.

"No."

He lifted a brow.

"Mine," she explained. "I keep waffling between guilt at lying to my family, thinking that I should just stop this madness and confess the truth."

"By *stop this madness* do you mean stopping . . . us?"

"Jaime," she said and sighed. "I like you. I really do. But I don't lie to my family." A shake of her head. "I never have, and to lie about something this big." She dropped her gaze to the floor. "I wanted the setups to stop, that's it."

The back of his throat burned, and he wanted to shout at her, to demand she acknowledge this, that *they* were more than just a lie.

But he needed to stay calm.

So, he gritted his teeth, sucked in a long, slow breath through his nose. One. Two. Three. Holding it in his lungs before releasing it just as slowly. Out. Two. Three.

Then he asked, "And the other thing?"

Her gaze came up, eyes sliding to his, questions in those whiskey depths.

He took solace in the fact that their hands were still laced together, squeezed her fingers lightly. "You said you were waffling," he murmured. "What was the other thing you were waffling with?"

Bright white teeth pressed into a lush, rosy bottom lip.

"Kate," he warned, using his thumb to free it, unable to stop himself from stroking his finger across the plump, lickable surface.

She shuddered. "God, I like it when you touch my lips like that."

He grinned. "Then keep biting them, and I won't be able to resist."

Her throat worked as she swallowed hard.

"*Kate.*" Another warning, one that had her eyes flashing with fire, annoyance entering her tone.

"You haven't earned the right to give me orders," she snapped.

He dropped his hands to her waist. "Well, then tell me what you're waffling with, Red. The lying to your family and what?"

A mulish expression on her face.

His fingers tightened.

Just slightly, but enough that he felt her shiver. So, his Red liked it when he gripped her hips. Not that he *didn't* like it. Hell, just putting his hands on her made his cock hard. Still, it was another piece of the Kate puzzle and as thus, he filed it away.

Along with the image of gripping those hips and thrusting deep.

"What, Red?" he asked again, forcing himself to focus.

"I'm torn between the lie and wanting what's between us to be real!"

It was a burst of noise, of words, and combined with her yanking out of his hold, of moving away from him, it took Jaime a second to process.

By the time he did, she was at the counter, shoving another pod into the Keurig.

"I—" *Slam.* The top went down. "Kate—" She kept her back to him and hit the button, the coffee popping and hissing. "I'm —" *Scrape.* The plate slid back onto the counter.

And that was about all of the interruptions he could handle.

He closed the distance between them, coming close just as she spun around, just as she began to speak. "I—"

He sealed his mouth over hers.

Stiff. She was stiff against him for a single heartbeat. Then she melted, hands coming around his neck, and kissed him back, her tongue a scalding brand, her luscious curves pressed close. He'd been dipped into a vat of molten steel, his body burning up from the inside out, boiling with need, his nerves firing, his cock hard and aching.

She pulled back, chest heaving.

"I want us to be real," she said. "I want it so fucking bad." Her fingers tightened. "I want it because you're nice and funny and kind and gorgeous. I want it because you seem to like me. I want it because you're sexy and kiss me like you think I'm the same." Her eyes drifted away. "But at the same time, I know I *can't* want it because it won't last."

Desire blazing through his mind, eliminating his brain cells, but he still managed to ask, "Why, honey? Why do you think we won't work out?"

She pulled back, and though it was difficult, Jaime made his hands release her.

A stumbling step away, a shaking hand pushing her hair off her face. But then her gaze was back on his, and the bleakness in it stole his breath. Because she'd already written their ending, even as they'd just barely begun.

Her words confirmed the sentiment.

"Because anytime someone says they want me, they never mean it."

That was a fucking punch to the gut.

"Red," he murmured.

Her eyes closed and he watched her shoulders lift and fall on a long, slow exhale. Then she spoke, and it was like her tone had taken a one-eighty. "Anyway," she chirped. "That's just reality in dating in this world of Tinder and technology. Everyone has a short attention span and is always thinking of the next great thing." A shrug, her hair whipping as she spun back to the coffee maker. "How do you take your coffee?" She giggled, and it wasn't gentle or sweet or anything like her normal husky laugh. The rough sound cut through him like a dull blade. "I'm guessing black because I've seen the hair on your chest in your pictures."

Since she was doing a damned good job at having her conversation by herself, Jaime just leaned against the island counter and crossed his arms.

Then waited.

"Or maybe one sugar." Another false giggle. "Because you're so sweet." She nudged the plate holding the pastries. "Or at least have a sweet tooth based on the sheer volume of sugar on this plate."

Kate picked up the plate, brought it to the island. She didn't look at him as she set it on the island, nor before she turned and went back for the mugs.

Nor when she then set those on the counter.

"Do you want the turnover or the scone?" she asked. "Because this pumpkin muffin is mi . . . *ne?*"

Her statement ended on a halting question.

No doubt because her eyes finally made it to his.

"Who hurt you?"

"Wh-what?"

"Who hurt you?" he repeated. "You keep talking about our end before we've even begun. I've told you, I'm not interested in ending anything, that you already mean something to me"—he uncrossed his arms, ran his knuckles over her cheek—"I want to prove that to you, but I won't be able to do it if you keep pushing me away before I can."

"Jaime," she breathed.

"I know," he said and took her hands in his, pressed them to his chest. "I know we're new. I know trust takes time to build. But I also can't prove that you mean something important and big and wonderful to me if you won't let me in." He slipped one arm around her waist. "Just crack the door, Red. Just the tiniest bit. Ride this wave with me. Let me in so I can show you."

She dropped her forehead to his collarbone. "I'm scared."

"I'm here," he murmured. "I've got you."

"But for how long?"

Forever.

That was what he wanted to say, to declare, to force her to believe.

But how could he say that? How could he possibly make her understand that when they were so new, when she'd clearly been so hurt?

When pushing her to open herself wide may expose those wounds to the air?

He couldn't.

He just needed to keep practicing patience, to keep showing her that he was there, that he wasn't like whoever had injured her heart, and hope that someday she would see that he was different and recognize he was worth the risk of dropping all of her barriers.

"Okay," he said on a long slow breath. "I get it. I understand and I'm not going to keep pushing you to tell me something you're not comfortable sharing." He touched her cheek. "You don't have to tell me who hurt you, but Red, can you just give me a chance? Can you just let us have some time to learn each other before you end us? We haven't we even had a chance to begin."

"Jaime," she breathed.

"Please," he said, aware that he was pushing, even though he promised he wouldn't, that he was making his own crack in her barriers and shoving himself through.

Less patience than persistence.

But he couldn't make himself stop.

The reason for that made itself clear when Kate and her kind soul gave generously again. The woman who'd cared about his pain in the car. The one who'd worried and texted in the night. The one who looked up at him gently and nodded, lifting her hand and pressing it against his cheek before she leaned close, brought her lips to his, and whispered, "okay."

Then she kissed him.

Sweetly. Gently. Kindly.

Even when she was scared, she gave. Even terrified, she'd cracked the door to her heart.

She'd thrown a lifeline to a begging man.

There was no fucking way he was going to waste that.

He was going to make damn sure he gave back.

FOURTEEN

Kate

SHE LAY in bed that night, hours after Jaime had left, hours after she'd eaten a delicious pumpkin muffin and he'd had an apple turnover.

Hours after she'd made a promise to herself to stop thinking about the inevitable end of her and Jaime and how she knew it would be more devastating to lose him than it had been to lose any other relationship. Hours after she'd decided to focus on enjoying the time they had left.

"Fuck," she muttered, punching her pillow and tossing and turning in her bed.

Her very expensive, supposedly the world's most comfortable pillow. Her pricey mattress. Her ridiculously overpriced linens that were cozy and fluffy and normally had her sleeping like a baby.

Well, like a baby that wasn't little Lacy, up at all hours.

But instead she was awake, the fucking broken record of fear and end cycling through her mind.

Jaime had gone into his clinic about an hour after they'd

eaten together, after cleaning the dishes and mugs, after putting his muscles to excellent work by digging a series of holes for the new plants she'd planned on purchasing later that day.

As a result, she continued to think of him the entire time she worked in the garden.

Hell, he never left her mind.

Not on the drive to the nursery, nor as she picked out plants and she wondered what type would be his favorite and if she got that extra flat of marigolds if she would be able to convince him to dig a few more holes.

She thought of him as she loosened the flowers from their pots, as she broke apart their roots and sprinkled in some plant food before tucking them carefully into the soil. She thought of his capable hands as she used her own hand to pat the dirt down, remembering how his had felt as they touched and stroked and caressed.

But when he'd called that night, she hadn't picked up.

She'd let it go to voicemail then had listened to the short and sweet message he'd left, telling her he was thinking of her, that he missed her and for her to call him back anytime, and if not that he'd try her the next day.

But she hadn't returned the call.

Hadn't texted.

Instead, she spent the day in worry.

No matter all the grandiose promises she'd made to herself and him.

"Ugh!" she groaned, hating this, hating she was so insecure when it came to her love life. She was a confident and capable woman in every other part of her life. Self-assured at work. Self-reliant when it came to her house, her car, her life. She could change a tire, fix a leaking pipe. She could pay her own bills. Hell, she had learned how to patch her own roof last year when a big storm had ripped off a few shingles and she couldn't get a roofing contractor out for a few days and hadn't wanted her dad on the roof.

She could troubleshoot her WiFi and set up her cable box.

So, why couldn't she be in a healthy fucking relationship?

Why did she need to lie to her family or feel inadequate?

Why couldn't she open her heart to a man who was so clearly wonderful?

Knock. Knock. Knock.

She jumped, panic swelling in her despite all of her home-ownership self-reliance. Because it was nearly ten at night, and someone was pounding on her front door.

Kate grabbed her cell from her nightstand, her baseball bat from the side of her bed—it added to her capable because she could swing that sucker like a big-leaguer—and started to make her way out of her bedroom.

She'd hide in a closet or slip out the back door and she'd call the police.

There. Plan. Done.

Knock. Knock. Knock.

It came again just as she stepped out of her bedroom, and she jumped, nearly fell down the stairs.

"Katie!"

She jumped again, but this time it was less fear and more startle.

Because she recognized that voice.

"Katie!"

Heidi.

One of her closest friends. They'd met in college. They'd bonded first over drinking too much and christening the porcelain goddess, and forever over nerding out about *all* the things—Hermione Granger and unicorns and board games and even gardening, though that was really more of Kate's wheelhouse.

The point was that her very best friend was at her house, and it didn't take a genius to know why.

She'd heard about Jaime.

Knock. Knock. Knock.

"Don't try to hide, my Katie girl," Heidi called. "I've brought wine and ice cream, and we *are* going to talk about it."

And because Kate knew there was no point in trying to ignore Heidi—her friend put persistence to shame—she headed down the stairs, flicked on the light in the hall, and opened the front door.

Heidi strolled in as though they were mid-conversation.

"You've been keeping secrets, college roomie," Heidi said with a tsk.

Kate groaned. "I don't want to talk about it."

"Good," Heidi said, flicking on the lights in the kitchen and making herself at home. It wasn't a surprise. They'd been in each other's lives for more than a decade, had lived together on more than one occasion—four years in college, four more until Kate had bought this house. Heidi had long ago moved beyond guest status and was firmly in the category of family.

Which is why she had little compunction opening up the cabinet that held Kate's wine glasses and pulling out two. Another quick movement had her locating the bottle opener, and in the next few seconds, she had two glasses poured and had set one in front of Kate.

"I need your advice."

Suspicion slid through her. "You're not going to ask—"

"You about your fake engagement?" Heidi finished for her. "Fuck, yes, I am, because clearly you've got something big going on, but as much I want to squeeze every last bit of information out of you"—she lifted her hands and demonstrated her apparently very capable squeezing ability—"I also know your stubborn face."

Kate frowned. "Stubborn face?"

"Yup." A nod. A wave of her hand at Kate's face. "Locked and loaded, front and center, insert other similar clichés here," she said. "Which is why I'm going to wear you down with my life drama, and then you'll dish on yours."

Kate sniffed. "You wouldn't make much of an evil genius, you know that, right?"

"Because I'm telling you my nefarious plan?" Heidi shrugged when Kate nodded then pointed at the wine glass. "You're already halfway through that one. Another and you'll tell me everything I want to know. Muahaha!"

Kate pushed the glass away.

Heidi snorted. "Yeah, right. It's your favorite. I know you won't be able to resist."

Kate made a face. One, because her friend was right—it was her favorite. An ice wine from a small winery in Utah of all places. Two, because it was expensive, and she would feel too damned guilty if she didn't drink it. Heidi wasn't hurting for money, but she worked really hard and had pulled way too many hours re-stocking shelves at the college bookstore to afford to make her way through school, way too many hours doing double shifts in order to pay off her loans for Kate to waste some of her best friend's hard-earned wages.

Kate's mom getting the beauty deal just before college was the only reason Kate hadn't been in the same boat.

She would have had the loans, the extra hours, the struggle.

Growing up without a lot of frills had taught her to appreciate the little things right along with the big—and no bills upon leaving school definitely qualified as big, same as the wine was a small luxury.

One that should be appreciated just as much.

One that had her scowling at her friend and taking another large sip.

Tart and sweet, with notes of berry, it was freaking delicious.

Probably why her friend was looking at her all smug and self-important. "If I have a hangover tomorrow," she muttered. "I'm blaming you."

"You know we're finishing this bottle, right?" Heidi brushed her fingers over Kate's forehead. "It's small, so just three glasses each."

"Three!"

A bop to Kate's nose. "Release the lines. We'll both be pleasantly drunk. I'll spill, you'll spill, we'll all spill."

Kate wrinkled her nose. "That sounds like a terrible childhood song."

Heidi grinned, picked up her own glass, and took a sip. "I quit my job today."

Since Kate had followed her friend's example by drinking some of her own wine, she nearly spit all that glorious, tasty deliciousness out.

Let it be noted that spit takes were not sexy.

She repeated, *they were not sexy*. Sighing, she mopped up what had dribbled down her chin with a kitchen towel, while managing to swallow the rest, and glaring over at her friend. Heidi shrugged, not an ounce of remorse in sight. Kate set her glass down. "Why would you quit?" she asked. "You loved working at Carbon."

Heidi was a molecular physicist whose field of study was the space between atoms.

Her friend had explained the significance of that to her on more than one occasion but had never been able to dumb it down enough for a layman, such as Kate. Heidi could talk about work to only one person in their group, and that was Kelsey, who was a brilliant engineer, had earned multiple degrees—

some just for "fun"—but even she couldn't begin to match her friend's expertise.

"It's not sexy enough for you and your advertising brain," Heidi had declared on more than one occasion, which was possibly true.

Okay, it was *mostly* true.

Once Heidi began down a tangent of how atoms were mostly empty space and the speed of the electrons orbiting them, Kate's brain shut down.

So, Kate might not understand the nitty-gritty of Heidi's job, but she understood her friend.

And her friend loved working for Carbon Industries.

Loved it so much that she'd turned down several lucrative offers for other biotech companies over the years.

Kate reached across and snagged her friend's free hand, held it tightly with both of hers. "Why, Heid?" she asked. "I thought you were really happy there, and I think it was only a week ago that you mentioned your grant money came through."

Hazel eyes lock on hers, and it was impossible to miss the sadness in their depths. "It did."

"So, what happened?"

Heidi made a face. "The climate has just been deteriorating over the last few months," she said. "You know we got bought out"—a pause, her gaze alighting on Kate's for a moment before she nodded—"well, all of a sudden every step of our lab process has to be run through our corporate liaison. The product side of the company wants to make sure R&D"—research and development and the department in which Heidi worked—"isn't wasting resources and money."

"Okay." Kate squeezed lightly. "That doesn't seem all bad."

"I didn't think so either." Heidi pulled her hand back and pushed to her feet, pacing through the kitchen. "The problem is that our liaison is never available. And when she is, she clearly doesn't understand science. It's only numbers and appearances, and it's so infuriating." She tossed up her hands. "I don't have the supplies I need because the grant money is all tied up in corporate, waiting for my freaking liaison to approve the orders. Beyond that, I can't get approval for my interns to get overtime so they can come in on the weekends or after hours to check our experiments because those are resources that HR refuses to approve because it's too expensive." She paced back, scooped up her glass, and took a large sip. "Never mind that all of that was built into my request when I wrote the grant and the funds are there—"

A sigh.

"I'm boring you."

Kate jumped to her feet and rushed over to her friend, hugging her close. "Absolutely not," she said. "I was just thinking that this is the first conversation I've had with you about your work where I could understand everything." She pulled back on Heidi's snort. "And I empathize. I know you worked hard on the grant, know that you were so excited to get it."

"Yeah," she said. "I was."

"I'm sorry."

"I know." Heidi made a face. "I'm really going to miss my lab."

"Are you . . ." Kate stopped, nibbling at her bottom lip, then figured she might as well just ask. She and Heidi had never hidden anything and if she didn't ask, she'd worry. "Are you going to be okay for a while without a job? Money wise?"

A nod. "I'm good, Katie girl."

Relief slid through her. "That changes, you let me know."

"Will do," Heidi said, "but I've already begun applying other places. Luckily, there aren't too many people who can do what I do. I know it won't take long to find something."

"Smarty-pants."

"*Liar* pants," Heidi countered with a lifted brow that seemed to say, "your turn."

"I haven't even finished my first glass of wine yet," Kate muttered, though there was hardly more than one drop left.

"Here." Heidi topped her off then did the same for her own drink. "Second glass commencing."

Kate pouted. "Bully."

"Assertive," Heidi said.

"Pain in my ass," Kate muttered.

Heidi nodded. "Damn right."

Kate sighed. "Annoying."

"You love me," Heidi sing-songed.

Kate *did* love her friend. So freaking much. Which was why she didn't want to admit what she'd done. Heidi would understand, but Heidi would also . . . understand too much.

She knew all about Kate's superpower.

"Can't we just pretend you didn't hear what you heard?"

"You mean, can't I just pretend that you're not fake engaged when your mom calls me and tells me we *have* to plan a surprise engagement party for you and the mysterious Jaime, and we have to do it fast?" Heidi shook her head. "No can do, babe. We can't pretend *that* didn't happen." A nudge of her shoulder against Kate's. "And you're damn lucky she called me first and I could write my shocked-into-silence off as distraction by something in my lab instead of her calling Kels or Cora first. They would have balked and spilled the beans, and you know it," she said, naming their other two closest friends. "I told her I would do a survey of everyone's availability and get back to her, but Katie . . . this is a big lie."

"I know." She tried to swallow down the guilt and asked quietly, "How'd you know it was a fake engagement?"

"Really?" Hazel eyes bored into her. "We all had dinner not

even a week ago, and you went on and on about how you were worried you'd be re-virginized because it had been so long." A roll of those eyes. "That convo ring a bell?"

Oh. Yeah. *That.*

"Pretty short courtship for a real fiancé," Heidi said.

"I—"

Heidi cut her off. "Why'd you do it?"

Kate made a face. "My mom was going to set me up again, and I just blurted something out. I didn't even really mean to say I was engaged. It just slipped out and then it was *out,* and she was so thrilled that I didn't know how to take it back and—"

A nod. "Thus, the lie grew."

Kate winced. "Yeah."

"So, who is he?" Heidi asked.

"*JaimeTheVet,*" she said.

Heidi blinked. "The Instagram guy with the man bun that you've drooled over for months?"

Kate nodded. "Though he doesn't have the man bun anymore. He cut it off because he didn't think my parents would approve of him having long hair."

"Really?" Heidi exclaimed. "But his hair was so nice—" She stopped herself midsentence with a wave of her hand. "That's not the most important conversational hurdle at this point. Did he teach you how to do that flawless bun?"—her gaze went to Kate's, who shook her head—"Damn. Okay, we'll circle back to that glorious hair later. The more important part of this story is that he doesn't know you, so why would he agree? Are you paying him?"

A shake of her head. "No," she said. "I messaged him after I talked to my mom. I knew it was an insane thing to do. I mean, I totally get that. But then I asked him, and he said yes, and we agreed to go to dinner on Thursday, and he was late because he was doing a procedure on a guinea pig with a heart problem, and then he held my hand, and we walked to the pier, and then he kissed me, and it was hands-down the best kiss of my life." She gulped down more wine. "I like him, Heidi. A lot."

"But does he like you?"

Ouch.

Kate dropped her stare to the granite, taking in the flecks of silver amongst the pale blue, blinking hard.

Does he like you?

That was the crux of all of her fears, wasn't it?

Did he like her, really? And if he did like her genuinely, would that like last? And if it lasted, would that lasting be days or weeks or months before he betrayed—

Heidi's hand covered hers. "I didn't mean it like that," she murmured.

Kate's throat burned, but she squeezed out. "I know."

"No," Heidi said, "I don't think you do." Her friend tugged the glass out of Kate's hands, gripped her wrists tight. "You are one of the best people I know. You're smart and funny and kind . . . even though you have a weird redheaded connection thing with Hermione Granger." Kate snorted. "You do," Heidi said, lips tipped up at the edges. "But I love you, and you're my fucking best friend, so believe me when I say that there is no person on this planet who deserves to have everything they want more than you."

"A big *but* is coming," Kate muttered.

"Yes," Heidi said. "Except, the but is that I don't want you to get hurt again."

Neither did she. It was why she kept throwing up barriers between herself and Jaime even though she really liked him. It was why her mind kept pulling her back even though her heart continued to encourage her further.

"He says he was drumming up the courage to ask me on a date when I messaged. That he took the opportunity to get to know me. He says he wants more dates and wants to prove that I can trust him." She sighed. "He says he knows that takes time, but that he can be patient. And—" Her gaze flicked to Heidi's. "He brought me breakfast and paid attention enough to know that my favorite breakfast is from Molly's, that I love mochas. And he's the oldest of four and is great with babies—he even managed to get Lacy to not have a meltdown for almost a half hour. Then he handled my mom and dad and brother and sister with aplomb and kindness. *And* he takes care of a rooster named Barry, who walks on a leash."

Chest heaving, she pulled out of Heidi's grip, shoved her hair out of her face.

"And I'm fucking terrified," she said, eyes burning. "Because I like him, too. Because this was just a stupid lie, and I hardly know him. Except, I *do* know him." She thumped a fist against her chest, just over her heart. "I know him here. From the moment I met him, it was like I had this connection to him. And not even all physical, because of course he's beautiful and sexy, anyone could see that. But because he-he's—"

"Different."

She glanced up at Heidi. "Yes. He's different."

"And you don't want to get hurt again."

"I've jumped into things with men too many times in my life, Heidi. I've thought they were all different, that they were all good, and when they didn't work out, I thought that it was just a matter of finding a man who could be the one. That I just needed to keep looking." She closed her eyes. "Then I realized that lightning doesn't strike in the same place over and over again. Then I realized it was me. I was the thing that connected us, and *I'm* the thing that's wrong in every relationship I've had." Another thump of her fist to her chest. "I'm the messed up one that makes everything implode."

"Well, that's bullshit."

Kate was so far down her proverbial mental rabbit hole that it took her a few seconds to realize what Heidi had said.

"*What?*" she exclaimed.

She'd just poured her heart out to her best friend, exposed her vulnerable underbelly, and confessed all of the twisted and sad things she'd been feeling, and Heidi had just called it all bullshit.

"I'm—"

Heidi's hand came up, palm out. "I heard you, Katie," she said. "Believe me. I heard every single fucking word and the absolute bullshit that is lacing them together. Yes, you might have been guilty of falling for people too quickly every once in a while, but who hasn't fallen harder than the person you're seeing and gotten hurt—"

"That's not what I mean—"

"And further that, maybe you've dated some freaking douchebags, but again, who hasn't?" Heidi said, talking over her. "Everyone I know has gone through plenty of assholes before they realized they wanted something more, something different."

"Except—"

"Except, what? You were stupid and didn't understand your worth?" Heidi took a sip of wine. "Welcome to the club. We've all been a little stupid in love now and then."

"I don't think I understand—"

Plink. The cup settled onto the granite. "I do, honey," Heidi murmured. "I do understand. You've done an A-plus job at picking losers, but I've also seen you with good men, but ones who just aren't compatible with you, personality or lifestyle or otherwise. That doesn't mean that there's something wrong with you. That makes you normal at this whole dating thing."

"Heidi."

"Steve Hollen."

"What?"

"He was a good guy. Nice. You saw him for three months. You two broke up because he moved to the East Coast. *Not* an asshole."

"I—"

"Berkeley Anders. Six dates. Good kisser. Fun to hang out with. But you stopped seeing him because he wanted to go out all the time and you wanted to be home more. Also, not an asshole."

"He—"

"Was a little hurt when you broke it off, yes, and didn't want to continue *being friends*." Heidi rolled her eyes. "That doesn't happen in real life, no matter how sweet you are inside. I know you joke about your asshole superpower, but you don't have one, Kate. What you *do* have is the ability to give glimpses to that big, wonderful heart of yours, but then to shut anyone out who wants to reach for it."

"That's not—"

"Fair? Maybe." Heidi shrugged. "But it's also true. A few months ago, Thompson Arnold. He was boring. Three dates. You never went on a fourth. Not an asshole. And if you want me to keep going, I can circle *all* to college. Keith Black. Senior year. Totally into you. Took you on at least ten dates and bought you roses and wanted to sync up on his post-grad with your internship so he could keep seeing you." Heidi walked over, held her stare. "Also, not an asshole, but you cut him loose."

Kate's pulse thundered, the memories surrounding her, memories she'd suppressed. Heidi and her list were right. She had seen Keith and Thompson and Berkeley and Steve and frankly *more,* but she'd never really let them in. "*I'm* the asshole," she murmured.

"No," Heidi said on a laugh. "You're not. You have that big heart, the one that draws everyone in, but you're really good at giving, at helping, at jumping in if someone has a crisis. You're great at loving everyone else." She tapped the spot over Kate's heart. "Except, yourself. Because as much as you give, you never really open yourself up enough to truly trust or rely on another person."

"I—"

"Trust on your family, your friends?" Heidi nodded. "Yeah, you do. But even then, you make it hard sometimes, babe. You want to take care of us, but if we try to help you in return, you do the capable thing and push us away."

"I'm not—" She broke off, eyes stinging.

"The hole in your roof Cora's brother offered to fix? Walking home when you got a flat instead of calling us? Being sick as a dog and taking care of yourself instead of calling me or your mom or Cora—"

"The baby—"

"I know, Katie," Heidi said gently. "There's always a logical reason for not. But . . . you need to think if it's really logic that's having you do it all yourself, having you help everyone else, but not accepting that same care in return."

Fuck. Kate had the sinking sensation her friend was right.

"I know you're not trying to hurt us," Heidi murmured, reaching for her hand. "I don't know why you think you have to do it all yourself when we have your back, will always have it, but I can get needing to hold things close to your chest." A squeeze. "But consider, I've known you for a decade-plus, and I don't understand why you build the walls, why you keep me out of the inner sanctum of your heart, so how can you expect to be comfortable enough to be in a relationship that deep?" A pause. "Or how do you really know you want that?"

Kate swallowed hard but couldn't find the words.

It didn't matter, because Heidi had them anyway.

"You have this mental block, babe. Always have. For some

idiotic reason, you think that what's inside you isn't valuable or important or grand enough for someone to love every single part —the good, the bad, the in-between." She brushed back Kate's hair. "And yet you don't hesitate to love the people around you, warts and all."

Kate's gaze slid away.

Heidi let her get away with that, but that didn't stop her from having the final word.

"It took me a long time to figure it out," she said, gently. "You give, Katie girl. You give so much that you don't have to risk taking." Heidi cradled her jaw, forced Kate to meet her stare. "You give so much because that means you don't have to open up those steel plates around your heart and actually let someone in to care for you in return. Because if you did, then you would be vulnerable."

Then with those words that pierced right through Kate's armor, she pressed a kiss to her cheek, pulled on her coat, and walked right out of Kate's house.

In like a hurricane, gale force winds knocking everything that Kate thought she knew into disarray, and then out just as abruptly, the aftermath she left behind heavy and silent and . . . shattered.

Sinking down to the tile, Kate buried her face in her hands.

And then she cried.

For a long, long time.

FIFTEEN

Jaime

HE KNEW SOMETHING WAS WRONG.

How he knew, he wasn't going to second guess.

But from the moment his eyes had slid open, the sun barely cresting the hills in the distance, he'd felt a deep pit of unease in his stomach.

Something was wrong with Kate.

Jaime didn't bother to hesitate or think through the instinct or take a moment to pause and remember they'd been fake fiancés, and something more, for less than a week—message to first date to family dinner. He simply got dressed and drove over to Kate's house.

She was sitting on her front porch, hair tumbled around her face, top of her body swallowed by a huge gray hoodie, patterned pajama pants swimming over her legs. But what had his stomach twisting itself into knots was the expression on her face. Bleak and exhausted, despite the mug filled with what he assumed was coffee that she was holding in her hands.

Maybe it would have been more prudent to keep driving, to

move past this woman who was beautiful and lovely and fun and not complicate his life.

But it wasn't even an option that crossed his mind.

He'd decided on this adventure, on this path that would hopefully gain him Kate's heart, her body, her soul linked to his from two minutes into that conversation at dinner. Hell, if he were being honest with himself, he'd decided on her from the moment that message had hit his inbox.

Such a random, odd request.

And also, one he'd never even considered denying.

It was probably stupid to have been infatuated with a woman he'd only known over social media, probably even more so to have fallen for her two minutes into their first date.

But there it was.

And he was riding it through to the end.

He was going to follow through with what he'd promised. He was going to show patience and perseverance and win the heart of the gorgeous, fun, amazing woman who was sitting so sadly on her front porch.

Decision made.

All in.

No waffling required.

Jaime got out, walked up the drive. Kate's gaze had fixed on his the moment he'd opened the driver's side door, and it stayed there as he moved toward her.

But when her lips parted as he approached the bottom step of the porch, he didn't give her a chance to speak, to find some piece inside her to push him away.

Instead, he snagged the mug from her grip, set it on the wood, and sat, picking her up and plunking her into his lap.

"Jaime," she whispered.

"Hush now," he said, stroking the hair off her face, seeing

how pale she was, the dark circles under each eye. He brushed his thumb along both. "You didn't sleep last night, Red?"

She shook her head.

"Because of me?"

Another shake.

"Then why, baby?"

Her eyes filled with tears, the tip of her nose went pink, and he had to struggle to contain the urge to want to pulverize whoever had hurt her when a single tear appeared at the corner of her eye and slid down her cheek. "Because of *me*, Jaime. I'm so messed up inside."

The pain in that statement made *his* eyes sting. "No, you're not," he argued. "You're wonderful and perfect and—"

Fingers on his lips, silencing his words.

"I *am* messed up," she said firmly, pressing harder when he sucked in a breath, prepared to disagree with her further. This woman meant more to him after a week than any woman had ever meant, his family aside. And he didn't want to kiss and touch and hold his mom or his sisters. He also certainly didn't want to sleep with them—*shudder*. Her next words took any of the light in his mind and smashed it to bits. "I'm so fucking broken and ruined and—"

She broke off on a sob, and he held her tight, mind spinning.

Her words aside, he'd thought of little else except for Kate for months now. First, imagining how he might get a shot with her, and now thinking of all the ways to keep her now that he finally got that chance.

And he'd be the first to admit that he clearly didn't know everything about her.

But he knew enough.

The biggest and most important piece of that *enough* was the fact that she wasn't messed up or ruined or broken.

Maybe she'd been hurt. Maybe she was scared. But that was normal.

He had his own fair share of old hurts and pain. "If I said I was damaged inside, if I had too much baggage inside to be in a relationship, what would you say?"

She glanced up, those pretty whiskey eyes damp, but her tone was impassioned.

"You are wonderful, Jaime," she said, straightening and gripping his shoulders. "You've been absolutely kind and amazing this week. So understanding. I feel so lucky that you didn't blow me off and—"

He closed the distance between their lips, pressing a short, firm kiss to her mouth.

When he pulled back, he asked, "Can't you see that I feel the same?"

She bit down on her bottom lip then sighed. "My best friend told me last night that I have walls up and that I give a lot in relationships, that I make such an effort to take care of my family and friends so I can control my relationships, so I can keep distance between myself and the people I love." She swallowed hard. "So I don't have to open myself up, don't have to take their kindness and risk letting them in. I stayed up all night, wanting to pretend I had no clue what she was talking about. To be mad and angry that she would even suggest something so asinine." Her eyes, dry now, drifted to his. "Then I realized she was right."

He held her a little closer, slid his hand up and down her back, tracing lightly, not wanting to interrupt, but also wanting her to know that he was there, that he was listening.

"It's safer to be the one that's giving more sometimes because then you don't have to be open to taking. Ugh! I'm doing the worst job of explaining what seemed so clear when Heidi said it." She groaned, pushed against his chest, and he released her, leaning back against the pillar as she got up and paced the porch. "It makes sense in my head, I guess. It's one thing to make yourself a martyr for other people, to give and *give* until there's nothing else and then everyone can say, *oh, that Kate is so wonderful and generous.*" She tucked her hair behind her ear. "But what they don't realize is that the giving has the power. I've spent so many of my relationships being the care-taker, planning all the things, making sure the person I was seeing had everything he needed, that I then didn't have to make room in my life for someone to look beneath the veneer. There was such a flurry of caring, of giving, of being in charge that I didn't ever have to be vulnerable to them." She sighed. "And because I was the one in control, it was easy for me to step back, to cut ties, to say they weren't giving me what I needed." Her eyes came to his. "Even if I never so much as gave them a chance to take care of me."

Jaime shoved to his feet, understanding now. She wouldn't make it easy to care for her, would push away those who tried. But he was good at caring, and he could be damned stubborn when it came down to it.

He touched her cheek. "You expected me to say no to the message," he said, and she nodded. "And more than that, I started caring for *you*, instead of the other way around."

She nodded. "I didn't even have a chance to build my walls because you were just there and inside and you keep doing all these nice things for me—" A sigh, her chin dropping to her chest. "And I don't know *how* to take." She threw her hands up. "I just don't know how and I keep thinking I need to make it up, to care for you instead and . . . I'm so fucking scared because it's been a week and I like it too damned much."

He crossed to her, pulled her against him.

Maybe this was another moment with a should have.

He should have lied. He should have molded the truth, softened the blow in order to make it so she wasn't scared.

But Jaime hadn't lied to Kate, hadn't minimized or reduced anything between them, and he damn sure wasn't about to start now.

"Good," he said, using one hand to cup her cheek, to force her to look at him.

"Good?"

"Yup." He kissed her again, short and fast and hard. "Because I don't care if you're scared, Kate McLeod. I like you and I like taking care of you and I'm not going to stop." He ran his thumb across her bottom lip. "You're stuck with me."

Her breath shuddered out.

"And a good relationship isn't about keeping distance or measuring all the nice things you do for your partner on a scale. It's not a tit for tat, I do something, you do something." He brought his other hand up, cupped her other cheek so that he held her face in his palms and her stare couldn't dart away. "Sometimes the scale tips one way. Sometimes the other. But it's okay if it's not perfectly balanced, or—" He kissed her forehead. "Or if that care is heavier in your direction for a bit. At some point in the future, it'll bounce the other way."

"But what if I can't let it?"

He smiled. "Good thing I'm stubborn and pushy."

A shaky laugh.

He nuzzled her throat. "You're stuck with me, Red," he said again, wanting to make it clear, even while knowing it would take her time to believe him.

"Jaime," she began.

"No, Red." Fingers on her cheeks, brushing away the tears that were falling in earnest. "You're stuck with me until you order me to go—" He paused, considered that. "You know what? Fuck it. Try to order me to leave. Try to run. Try to push me away, but you'll still be stuck with me." A shrug. "Because you're the most incredible woman I've ever met, and now you inched open that door. I'm not stepping back. I'm not backing off. I'm pressing forward." Another kiss, gentler this time, his next words equally so. "I'm going to make my way through the rest of that armor, baby, and once I get to your heart, I'm going to keep it safe because it will be *here*." He took her hand, pressed it to his chest. "Because it's going to be so tightly bound to mine that I'll always be there to protect it."

He kissed her tears from her cheeks, slipped one arm around her waist to hold her tight.

"You know I'll want to protect your heart, too?" she asked, determination on her face.

Love swelled in him, because that was the Kate he was growing to know. Generous and sweet and so fucking incredible that she was absolutely worth fighting for.

"It's already yours to protect, Red."

And then he let his lips drop to hers and kissed her.

He kissed her until the sun rose fully.

He kissed her until her stomach rumbled.

Then he bought her breakfast.

And then . . . well, then he kissed her some more.

SIXTEEN

Kate

IT WAS TUESDAY NIGHT.

She was still feeling vulnerable, and Jaime was still being wonderful.

He'd bought her breakfast on Sunday after she'd turned into a sobbing fool then had spent the day in her garden with her, digging holes, stealing kisses, and then insisted on paying for the dinner they'd had delivered.

He hadn't argued when she'd said she was making him cookies, though—her way of evening the scales. Yes, she knew, or at least was coming to understand that, logically those scales didn't need to be balanced, but she couldn't just take all the time, she needed to give, to care. She just promised herself that she wouldn't use it as a way to keep her distance.

She would care for Jaime because he was lovely and sweet and it made her happy to see the soft way he looked at her when he'd stolen a scoop of raw dough—and the faux wounded expression when she'd smacked his hand, warning him off because the raw eggs and uncooked flour, and then he'd teased her into a "dangerous" kiss.

And she didn't protest when he'd cleaned the bowl and utensils she'd used to prep the dough because he had already stolen way too many hot circles of deliciousness off the baking sheets after they were baked and before they were fully cooled. He'd laughed when she'd teased and said there was no way he was going to keep his abs flat if he kept that up.

"I think you'll still like me even with a keg," he'd said, stealing a kiss that tasted of dark chocolate and brown sugar.

Because that much was true, she'd kissed him back, slow and deep and—

Had stolen the rest of his cookie. Which had gained her another teasing kiss, another bite of the treat, and plenty of laughter, soothing the tears in her heart, but instead of blocking them off with steel or barring the entrance to the door that had cracked, Kate had resisted the urge to retreat.

She'd stayed open.

And had received another yummy mouthful for her trouble.

And *that* was something she couldn't say around Heidi for fear of dirty-mindedness teasing.

Aw, who was she kidding? Just thinking about it two days later still made her giggle.

Anyway. Moving on.

So, after they'd finished with their Cookie Battle Royale, they'd watched a movie, cuddled on the couch, and he'd said goodbye with a sweet kiss that had left her wanting more.

Monday had been crazy for them both.

She had the usual weekend catch up and he had back-to-back clients, but Kate had pushed herself a bit, too. She'd called him after a particularly trying meeting with a client, let him tease her into a lighter mood with promises of more carbs and kissing and a way to work off the "keg."

Not keeping him at a distance.

Plus, there was little fucking hope of that now. He'd seen the blubbering. He'd listened when she'd explained. He'd . . . stayed.

And after the cheer up call, she'd sent *him* lunch.

A salad he'd mentioned he liked from Molly's—which proved that the man had good taste and might keep his abs yet.

She wasn't entirely vain, didn't begin to think that her body was anything close to perfect. She'd just . . . like to trace those lovely squares once.

Okay, once with her fingers.

And once with her tongue. Maybe twice.

"Focus," she murmured, waving to her sister and Dave as she bounced little Lacy on her shoulder. She had been pleasantly surprised that Ann had called and asked if Kate was still up for watching Lacy so she and Dave could go to dinner.

Of course, she'd said yes, but paired with that affirmative was the realization that perhaps the taking care of everyone and everything around them, sometimes to the detriment of themselves, was a McLeod female trait. Their mom had certainly never taken time for herself. Her whole life had been her work and family, and more often than not, her work had bled over into family—interns staying at their crowded house when their air conditioning went out in the middle of a heatwave, a visiting colleague coming for dinner, endless piles of paperwork stacked on her dresser and nightstand to be completed after the kids went to bed.

Kate's dad worked hard and loved them all.

But she didn't think he comprehended the extra burden her mom carried. Or maybe . . . it was part missing the signs and part those barriers that hid that heavy load.

"Damn," she murmured, waving until they were out of sight before slipping inside and closing the door behind her. This being aware of and trying to ferret out understanding of her emotions wasn't for the faint of heart.

Luckily for her sister, it seemed that Dave was beginning to understand that extra weight Ann was shouldering.

And she was beginning to be able to communicate her needs.

Who said McLeods couldn't learn?

Grinning, Kate thought of Ann tugging Dave's hand when he'd lingered, clearly already missing Lacy, and saying they needed to go because she wanted to be able to have an adult conversation with her husband over food that wasn't from a box or stone-cold because it had been interrupted by a little monster who was absolutely adorable but had terrible timing.

She ran her finger down Lacy's nose, giggling softly when she wrinkled it and squirmed slightly. "They'll be okay," she murmured. "I think your Mommy is a lot less stubborn than your Auntie when it comes to matters of the heart."

Lacy squawked. Kate giggled again. And then she went into the kitchen, ready to start her girl's night.

Jaime had offered to bring her dinner when he stopped by her office that afternoon on the way to a house call for one of his elderly clients—and yes, she was grinning when she remembered that she had a man in her life who stopped by her office, one who'd made her coworkers' jaws drop open because he was so handsome—but she'd seen the circles under his eyes, knew he'd been slammed the last two days.

So, she'd kissed him and sent him on his way, told him they could have a sexy conversation when he was tucked snugly in bed.

"Promise you'll tell me what you're wearing?" he'd asked, sliding his hands through her hair and making a shiver skate down her spine.

"Only if you promise to do the same."

A smiling kiss, and then he'd gone.

And now she had a sexy phone call to look forward to. "Maybe," she murmured, walking Lacy around the kitchen as she scrounged some ingredients for dinner, "I'll even get a sexy FaceTime."

Lacy cooed.

Laughing, she held the tiny bundle of cute and threw together a sandwich and some fruit, not feeling capable enough at the whole cradling a fragile infant and cooking at the same time.

As those things went, she managed to eat exactly one bite of her sandwich before Lacy stopped being adorable and sweet and fun and turned into an angry, crying beast.

Just kidding.

Sort of.

She got hungry. And when Lacy got hungry, she got Mad.

Yup. Mad with a capital M.

Kate bustled over to the fridge, grabbed the bottle of milk Ann had left for her. But what Kate didn't have was a fancy bottle warmer like her mom and sister had on their counters.

She had to rely on her old babysitter tricks.

And they were a hell of a lot slower than the fancy warming contraption.

God, who knew it took water an eternity to boil? Or what felt like one anyway, when there was an unhappy baby in her arms. An unhappy baby who wasn't shy about letting her unhappiness be known to the room.

The house.

The universe.

Snorting as she kept moving, trying the pacifier and rocking and singing and talking and bouncing and anything else she could think of in order to distract Lacy—none of which made the least bit of difference—she wasn't exactly pleased to hear the doorbell.

Pulling the pan of boiling water off the heat, she plunked the bottle into it and hurried to the door, turning the handle just as the bell rang again.

She tugged it open, saw Jaime on the other side.

"Sorry," he said over Lacy's crying, lifting a hand and gently tucking a strand of hair behind her ear. "I didn't think you heard over her."

Kate nodded, turned and kissed his palm. "It's okay." She stepped back, inclined her head to the kitchen. "I've got to grab her bottle."

"Here. Let me take her."

They made the switch, and she bustled into the other room, snagging the bottle and quickly testing the temperature, before screwing on the nipple and walking back over to Lacy and Jaime.

Lacy, who'd stopped crying.

Lacy, who was looking up at Jaime adoringly.

For God's sake, the man was good.

"Do you want me to—?" She began.

"I can," he murmured, rubbing slow circles on Lacy's back. "Unless you want to."

Lacy had stopped crying. Kate wasn't messing with that. She passed over the bottle. "It's all yours, baby whisperer." He glanced up and smiled, and for the first time since she'd seen him on the front porch, she realized that there were shadows in his eyes. She touched his jaw. "Jaime," she murmured. "Are you okay?"

All trace of amusement faded, and a flash of pain slid through his pale brown eyes. "I'm fine."

"Hey—"

Lacy began to cry in earnest, and he smiled, repeated, "I'm fine."

But she'd seen that glimpse of hurt.

And this was a moment she could give as well as take. Give care. Take some of his pain, his burden, whatever he was carrying that day that was weighing so heavily on him.

Because the man talked a good talk about getting Kate to take *his* care, about out-stubborning her into it if he had to, but now she saw he needed a taste of his own medicine.

He needed to accept that she was damned well going to do the same for him.

First, though, Lacy needed to be taken care of.

Then she was going to find some freaking courage—and hold on to it—and she was going to keep the door cracked while she took care of Jaime.

Not put up barriers while helping him.

Not pulling back.

Because one thing had become crystal clear to her over the last week—she wanted a different future. Not so scared that something was going to go wrong at some hereto unknown point coming down the road that she missed out on all the great things in the now.

Lacy quieted, the sound of sucking filling the space, and Kate took the opportunity of free arms to start pulling ingredients out of the fridge. "Have you eaten?" she asked.

Silence.

Frowning, she turned, saw that he was watching Lacy, but he didn't really seem to be all there.

"Jaime?" she asked.

He jerked slightly. "Sorry, what?"

"Are you hungry?"

A slow blink as he processed her question, and that more than anything told her that her instincts were right.

He was as good as her about giving care.

And as bad as her about accepting it.

Give *and* take. They both needed practice at it.

"Yeah, Red," he finally said, "I'm hungry."

"Okay, baby," she murmured, and went back to gathering up supplies to whip up a quick dinner. Her sandwich and fruit wouldn't fill him up, so she wrapped it and stuck it in a lunchbox for the next day. Then she pulled out a Tupperware of pasta sauce she'd swiped from her mom's freezer not long before, some fresh pasta she'd grabbed at a farmer's market near her office earlier that day. More water into the pot before putting it back on the heat. While that was heating, she grabbed a loaf of bread she'd picked up at the same market and sliced it then threw together a quick salad.

By that time the water was boiling, and she tossed the pasta in.

Five minutes later the pasta was cooked, some sauce was slapped on top, and she had two plates with dinner on them.

Nothing fancy, but tasty and she even got some veggies on.

Jaime paced back in, the bottle empty, and she winced when she saw a spot on his shoulder. Ann had mentioned a burb cloth in the diaper bag, but she'd been too frazzled by Lacy being hungry and Jaime arriving.

He met her gaze. "What is it?"

She crossed to him, paper towel in hand, and wiped off the spit-up. "Sorry," she said. "I forgot about the burp cloth."

The bottle hit the counter; his free arm wrapped around her waist. "Do you know the kinds of things I've had on this shirt?" he asked lightly, brushing a kiss to her forehead. "Thank you for cooking. It smells delicious."

She shrugged. "It's nothing."

Hand sliding up her back, fingers running over her jaw. "It's something to me." Eyes locked on hers. "Thank you."

Kate was still for a heartbeat, taking in the warmth, soaking in the way he stared at her. He saw her, saw what was inside her, and he was still there.

The door creaked open a little further.

And she managed to resist the urge to slam it closed, to throw every lock. "You're welcome," she murmured, and took his arm, bringing him to the table so he could eat.

Which proved difficult with one arm.

"Here," she said, snagging his fork and scooping up a bite, holding it to his mouth. "I think Lacy's trying to say you need to go on a diet," she teased.

He chuckled but parted his lips and let her feed him the pasta.

"Do you want me to take her so you can eat?" she asked after she'd fed him two more bites.

Warm brown eyes. "I like just what you're doing." A beat. "So long as you feed yourself, too."

A flush crept into her cheeks, but she nodded, even though she suddenly felt shy. The moment hadn't felt intimate before, but with him so close, with that hot gaze on her, she took abrupt notice of exactly what she was doing.

Feeding him.

Fingers on her cheek. "I do like it when you blush. Whatcha thinking, Red?"

Since she wasn't a ninny, she lifted her chin and said, "What I'd like to feed you in bed."

Heat flared, his lips parted, and a soft groan filled the air. "Killing me, Red."

Feeling quite pleased with the obvious hunger in his gaze, she smiled and scooped up a bite of pasta, before chewing and swallowing. "I was thinking of chocolate sauce," she said quietly. "But I figure that would be messy, and I really love my sheets."

His jaw fell open then he laughed, startling Lacy into tears. He stood and rocked her, managing to soothe her quickly, and leaned over to kiss her. "Sorry, little one, your Auntie Kate is funny," he murmured, brushing a kiss over her soft, brown hair, and when she settled down, he sat back down next to Kate. "Thank you," he said, warm eyes on her again.

"For what?"

He shook his head.

She reached over, took his hand. "Jaime," she murmured. "I'm trying here, trying to accept your care, but you need to accept mine, too." A squeeze. "If you want to be in my heart, you have to let me into yours, too."

Soft brown eyes on hers. "You saying I'm being stubborn?"

A brush of her fingers on his arm. "I'm just saying it takes a stubborn to know a stubborn." A beat. "But seriously, I need you to let me take care of you, too, okay? I need to tip the scales as often as you do."

He turned his palm over, captured her hand, and brought it up to his mouth. "Okay, Red."

Her heart swelled. "So, what were you thanking me for, baby?"

He didn't deny her this time, just held her hand and said, "For making me laugh when I didn't think that would be possible today."

She set down the fork she'd been using. "What happened?" she asked. "You didn't seem sad earlier at my office."

The warmth fled, cold filling the depths of his eyes. "My last house call didn't go well."

Reaching over, she squeezed his leg. "Tell me what happened."

He covered her hand with his, sighed. "I don't normally make house calls, but this woman has been one of my clients from the very beginning. She has some health problems, and it's been harder for her to come in for appointments. Her dog, Charlie, hasn't been well either."

The quiet and careful way he said that made her stomach clench.

"Turned out Charlie was doing worse than either of us realized," he said, continuing the quiet recital. "He was struggling to breathe, was septic, and his heart was failing." He sighed. "I had to . . . it had to be done today."

"Oh, Jaime," she murmured, hugging him as well as she could with a sleeping baby between them. "Oh, honey, I'm so sorry. I know that has to be so hard."

He nodded, brushed his lips against her temple.

And her heart clenched.

She pulled back. "That's not it, is it?"

"No."

"What, baby?"

"Margaret was so upset she started having chest pains."

Kate gasped.

"She's okay," he said quickly. "But I had to call an ambulance, and they took her in for monitoring while I took care of Charlie. Her grandson is with her now, and she's going to stay the night."

Carefully, she lifted Lacy out of his arms and carried her to the playpen she'd bought when her niece was born.

Of course, this was the first time Ann had left Lacy, so she'd never used it.

Luckily, Lacy didn't stir when Kate set her down, and she was able to walk back over to Jaime and do what she'd wanted from the moment she'd first noticed the shadows in his eyes.

She straddled his thighs, sat down in his lap, and hugged him tight. "I'm sorry."

He was stiff for a long moment then released a shuddering breath and wrapped his arms tight around her in return.

They held on to each other tightly and for a long time.

And . . . give and take.

Yes. *This* was give and take.

Jaime coming in and not hesitating to help her with Lacy, just stepping up and doing what needed to be done. And . . . Kate doing the same, seeing that he was hurting and offering comfort.

It was Jaime holding her when she realized a painful truth about herself.

And Kate making him dinner when he was hungry.

Give.

Take.

Give.

Take.

Love.

Yes, that, too.

SEVENTEEN

Jaime

ANN DIDN'T SEEM surprised to see him standing in the hall when they knocked and didn't waste any time in bundling Lacy into her car seat.

Dave took the infant seat out to their SUV in the driveway and snapped it in place while Ann got the recap, smiled at Jaime, and then disappeared with a wave and a coy, "You two have fun."

Then she was gone, looking lightyears happier than at the family dinner on Friday.

"They seem to have sorted out their trouble," he said, once the door was closed and their car had driven down the road.

"Yes," Kate murmured. "They'll be okay."

"McLeod intuitiveness?" he asked.

"Maybe stubbornness," she murmured, and brushing a kiss to his cheek. "You okay, baby?"

It had been a shitty afternoon and early evening but hearing her call him *baby* made it better. Same as Kate not getting mad, even though he'd known she'd needed space and patience and that she'd had plans watching Lacy.

He hadn't the strength to stay away.

But she welcomed him in. She'd cooked and fed and held him, and when he'd felt like the events of the afternoon had loosened their stranglehold, he'd managed to set her away from him long enough to do the dishes.

God, the way she looked at him when he washed a couple of plates.

Fuck.

He knew he'd just signed up to do them for the rest of his life, and he somehow didn't give one damn. Because he loved this woman and it made her happy.

Now she cuddled close to his side, tugged him back to the couch.

"Are you ready for your punishment?"

Jaime blinked. "What?" Were there more dishes to be washed?

"Your punishment," she said again and wound her arms around his neck, brought her body flush to his. "You knew I was having a girl's night and intruded anyway." A shake of her head. "Tsk. Tsk. So rude."

He grinned. "I think you need to consider that I saved the day."

One brow arched up. "Oh, really?"

"Yup," he said. "You needed my Lacy calming abilities, otherwise you'd still be heating that bottle and eating an apple for dinner."

"I'll have you know that apples are delicious," she said, lips tipping up at the corners. "And I took an advanced babysitting course in high school. It's how I was able to pay for my first car."

He chuckled. "Impressive."

"Yes," she said. "It is. I was the most sought-after sitter in our neighbor."

Jaime ran a finger down her cheek. "So, what you're saying is that I'm in the presence of greatness?"

She giggled. "Yup. That's *exactly* what I'm saying."

"Mmm." He trailed his fingers down her throat, stroked across one collarbone and then the other. "And what should I do with all that greatness?"

"Take me to bed?"

His jaw dropped open.

Her smile took his breath away. "Is that a yes?"

Fuck yes, it was a yes. Except, what if she was trying to make him feel better because he'd had a terrible day? What if she didn't really want this? What if she felt pushed into—

Her hands rested on his shoulders, kneaded lightly.

"This isn't a pity offer," she said. "You have to take your care medicine, same as me."

"Kate," he began. "I don't want you to feel like you have to—"

"Have more orgasms?" she interrupted, pressing closer. "Because, I mean, I know I don't *have* to have them." She smiled, and it took his breath away. "But I'd really *like* to have some, and I'd especially like to have them courtesy of you and not my vibrator."

He grinned. "Yeah?"

She nibbled at her bottom lip.

He groaned, used his thumb to release it, to soothe over the small hurt. "You know what that does to me, Red."

"Tell me." She ran her hand down his chest, his abs, gripped his waist. "Or better yet, *show* me."

And Jaime forgot about the teasing, the banter, pushed away the tough day, only pausing to mentally tuck the dinner and how she'd held him tight into a safe place in his heart, a place where he would never forget the memory of her arms around him, and then . . . he gave in.

He closed the distance between their mouths and kissed the woman he loved. One touch, and her lips parted. A heartbeat passed, and their tongues tangled. She moaned, fingers clenching on his waist, nails digging into his skin, sharp bites that made heat scald down his spine, whiskey trail down his throat, warming him from the outside in and the inside out in equal measure.

She jumped and he scooped her up, coaxing her to wrap her legs around him, breaking apart only long enough to ask, "Bedroom?"

A slow, sexy smile that turned his cock to granite.

"Up the stairs. Second door on the left. But I can wa—" She broke off on a moan when he nipped at her lip, when he kissed and sucked his way down her throat. Then he got his ass in gear, carrying this wonderful woman upstairs, down the hall, through the door, and dropping her onto the mattress.

He stopped only to step out of his shoes, to tug hers off her feet, but that was long enough to notice the bedspread. A grin stretched his lips. "Purple."

"Told you it's my favorite."

"Guess you weren't lying."

She crooked a finger, beckoning him closer when all he wanted to do was look his fill of this sexy woman before stripping her bare. But . . . he knew he had no hope of denying her anything, and so Jaime closed the distance between them, crawling up the mattress, reveling in how fucking good it felt to have her beneath him.

"What is it, Red?" he asked, pressing a kiss to her throat, her jaw, the space behind her ear.

Turning her head, she pressed a kiss to *his* ear and whispered. "I have purple other places, too."

Desire burned a trail down his spine, made his cock somehow get even harder.

But all he said was, "Yeah?"

A leg around his hip, a gorgeous smile on that kissable mouth. She took his hand, pressed it to her breast. "Yes." Slid it down the soft curves of her stomach, stopped just above the button of her jeans. "And yes."

His vision hazed, his fingers flicked open the button, then paused. "You sure, Red?"

"God, I like you," she said.

"Kate, I like you, too," he said. "In fact, I lo—"

Then she kissed him, cutting off his sentence. Which was probably for the best, because he knew he needed to remember that patience, knew they'd made big steps, and he didn't want to fuck it up.

Breaking away when his lungs screamed for air, he reached for her, but she batted his hand away, grabbed the hem of her sweater and shimmied it up and over her head,

And . . . Jaime had no words.

She was pale skin and amethyst lace. She was lithe, feminine curves. She was his every fantasy come to life. Freckles dotted her abdomen, her chest like a complicated roadmap that he was absolutely desperate to taste, to trace with his tongue. He wanted to chart every mark, to worship every inch.

Then she took his hand and brought it back to the top of her jeans. "Now, baby. Please."

There was no denying her anything.

He undid the zipper.

"Fuck, Red." Because there was more purple lace, the softest abrasion against his fingertips, damp heat radiating through the fabric, coating his skin. His mouth watered, remembering the taste.

They hadn't had dessert.

Well, he wanted it now.

Pushing off of her, he snagged her jeans at her ankles, tugged the fabric off her legs. A quick jerk had her panties going by the wayside, and a heartbeat later, he was between her thighs, that fucking glorious pink pussy an inch away from his tongue.

He didn't wait, didn't tease.

He licked her up and down, suckled on her clit, exactly as she liked. She'd been wet before he touched her, and the caress of his tongue, the pressure on the bundle of nerves had her moaning, moisture pooling. She was sweet with a hint of tart and by far the best dessert of his life. But as good as she tasted, he wanted her coming on his mouth, wanted her limp with pleasure, her eyes heavy and hooded.

So, he got to work.

One finger circling the entrance to her body, dipping inside, his tongue alternating between circling and pressing firmly. He showed no mercy. Instead, he used what he'd learned the other night and put it to pitiless use.

Not that she seemed to mind.

Her fingers wove into his hair, holding his mouth tightly against her as her hips bucked and ground and she rode his face.

It didn't take long for her to throw her head back, for her to cry out his name as she broke apart around him, pussy convulsing on his finger, liquid drenching his tongue, every muscle in her body going absolutely tense for one long moment.

Then she melted.

Fingers releasing his hair, arms falling limply to the mattress, eyes shut, chest heaving.

"Damn," he murmured, pressing a kiss to the inside of her thigh. "I didn't even get to your glorious breasts yet."

Her eyes slit open, warm pools of heated whiskey.

And then she laughed, a hot, breathy sound. "I don't know if

I can handle you getting"—she did a limp attempt of one-handed air quotes—"to my breasts."

He kissed her navel, nipped at her hip, her bottom rib, flicked his tongue over the tiny silver charm hanging in the middle of that purple bra. "I think I called them glorious breasts," he said. "And I'd disagree. I think you can handle anything I dish out." He slipped his finger under the elastic band, traced left and right, the barest brush to those luscious curves.

"Wish"—he slid higher, grazed a nipple—"ful thinking."

"Mmm." He sucked one hard point through the lace. "No, Red, it's not." He reached beneath her, flicked open the clasp and peeled the fabric away. "I *know* you can handle anything I throw your way."

Her eyes locked with his, her hand came up, fingers lacing through his hair.

Then she smiled. "I think I can, too."

And Jaime felt like fucking Superman.

He tossed the bra to the side, slanted his lips across hers and poured every ounce of love he had for this woman into the kiss. She was incredible, and he wanted her to know it, to pour her generosity back into her, to touch and hold and *please* her as she deserved.

He slid his hand up her side, cupped the soft globe of her breast, massaging the tissue gently before he tore his lips from hers and moved down her body to suckle her nipple deeply.

Those fingers tightened in his hair, her hips bucked, and she moaned loudly.

A moment later, however, she was pushing him away.

"I'm—"

"Get naked," she demanded. "I want to feel your skin against mine."

Jaime paused, considered that, but since he wanted to feel

her, too, since he wasn't opposed to all that silken skin rubbing against him, he obliged, pushing off her, yanking his T-shirt over his head, stepping out of his pants.

But when he would have left on his boxer briefs, she stopped him with a foot to his chest.

"No, baby," she said, reaching over her shoulder and tugging a condom out of the nightstand. "I want *all* your skin."

Sparks of desire prickled down his spine, through his finger-tips. He clenched his jaw until it throbbed, grasping for control, but he was desperate to feel some of the molten heat he'd had on his tongue spread out on his cock, coating the skin as he sank deep again and again and *again.*

Slow. Steady.

Her foot dropped. Her fingers wrapped around his cock. She sat up and . . . he felt a different kind of heat. Her lips closed over him, tongue stroking from base to tip.

And he forgot all about slow and steady.

He forgot all about anything except how good it felt to be in her mouth.

She squeezed tight, hand following the path of her tongue. Once. Twice.

His control splintered. He plucked her off him, tossed her back against the pillows, and he kissed her while stroking every inch of her he could reach. Caressing her breasts, rolling her nipples between thumb and forefinger, stroking over her waist, her hips, slipping his hand down into the damp heat, teasing her clit until she writhed against him in feminine complaint.

"Now!" she gasped, pulling her mouth away and grabbing for the condom, all but shoving it against his chest.

One more stroke of that bundle of nerves. One more breath-less moan.

And he took the condom, tore it open with his teeth, rolled it down the length of his cock. He shifted, positioned himself over her, and then stopped, met those gorgeous whiskey eyes. "Yes?"

Her face went soft. Her arms wrapped around him and she pulled him closer. "Yes, baby."

Jaime slid home.

Nothing had ever felt more right. He pushed in, bottoming out, feeling her clench tight around him, and he knew there would never be anyone else. That this woman had been built solely for him and he solely for her.

He pulled out slowly and moved back in, finding the rhythm she liked, gauging every moan and movement and flicker in those warm eyes.

He used that knowledge ruthlessly, not stopping until her breathing faltered again, until her fingers clenched, and her hips met his stroke for stroke. And still he moved, disciplined in that rhythm, needing to feel her break apart around him so that he could gather up the pieces and glue them back together.

Her head fell back, her legs convulsed, a moan rent the air.

Jaime lost his discipline. He lost everything except the feelings of the moment, of moving in and out, of tight and hot, of Kate wrapped around every inch of him.

Fire licked over his skin.

Desire pooled in his stomach.

His muscles clenched. His nerves were ablaze.

One thrust. Another. He exploded.

Pieces of him scattered every which way, but she was there. She held them tight as he flew right over the edge and shattered into a million shards.

And she caught every piece.

EIGHTEEN

Kate

HER FRIENDS WERE GLARING at her.

But she found she couldn't find the energy to care. Not when she had the gloriousness of last night under her belt . . . or rather *in* her—

"Always the quiet ones," Heidi said with a smirk.

Kate blushed and quickly shoved away all thoughts of how *in* Jaime had been.

Cora nudged Kelsey with her elbow. "Put down your phone and ignore Tanner's lovey-dovey texts. I know he's awesome and you guys are in luuuuv, but give us single girls a break, mm'kay?"

Kels rolled her eyes but shoved her phone into her pocket. "I was actually texting Angie. She was going to come tonight, but apparently her paper writing isn't going well."

Heidi made a face. "You know she likes those hockey girls better than us."

Kelsey chuckled. "She likes us fine," she said about their friend who was married to the professional hockey player Max

Montgomery and who worked with Kels at RoboTech. Angie had gone back to school to get her master's degree and while she didn't hang out as often as the core group of the four of them, hadn't gelled instantly like she and Heidi and Kels and Cora, Angie was fun and likable and popped in often enough that Kate considered her one of hers. "But it *is* probably easier for her to hang with the Gold hockey peeps. They're all on the same schedule *and*"—Kels's eyes narrowed onto Kate's—"there are no fake engagements."

Kate gulped. "It's not like that."

Heidi rolled her eyes. "It's *exactly* like that."

"Fine," she muttered. "It's like that a *little* bit." She held her finger and thumb up just slightly.

"Are you or are you not engaged?" Kelsey pressed.

It was Kate's turn to make a face. "I am not."

"Why is this giving me *Pride and Prejudice* vibes?" Cora asked. "Lady Catherine de Bourgh comes in and demands to know the status of your engagement to the prideful Mr. Darcy." Cora fluttered her eyelashes, pretending to swoon back onto the couch. "And our heroine lifts her chin, says in a firm voice, *I am not.*"

"Dork." Heidi punched her lightly in the shoulder.

"Yup." A shrug. "So, what?"

"Okay," Kelsey said. "I would really like to get back to the whole reason why Kate felt the need to pretend to be engaged to . . ." Her brows drew together. "To who exactly?"

Kate bit her lip, not wanting to say.

Her friends wouldn't judge her. Okay, they *would*, but it was out of love. Copious amounts of teasing and a smidge of judgment. But it came less from her friends' being jerks and more from them wanting the best for her.

Which meant that she understood their reticence with the whole fake engagement thing.

Typically, perpetuating a giant lie to her family with some fantasy guy she'd been lusting over on Instagram wasn't the most ideal start to a relationship.

But . . . it wasn't like that.

Not that she had the chance to explain how exactly *it wasn't like that* because Heidi took it upon herself to chime in.

"*JaimeTheVet*," she chirped.

Cora gasped. "With the man bun?"

Kate shook her head. "He cut it off because he was worried my parents wouldn't like it." She shrugged, lips twitching when Kels and Cora gasped. "Then he said he'd been meaning to get around for a haircut but was too busy."

Cora moaned. "But that hair." She jokingly swooned again. "So many guys with long hair look gross, like the strands are greasy and tangled and—" She shuddered. "*JaimeTheVet*'s was . . ."

"Glorious," Kels said, "and I hate everything about man buns simply on principle."

Heidi nudged her. "Or maybe it's because you're hopeless at doing hair?"

Kels wrinkled her nose. "Maybe that, too." She turned back, pinned Kate in place with a stern look. "But that doesn't explain why. Why pretend? You're a smart, capable woman who could easily date someone for real and—"

"My mom was going to set me up again." Kate sighed. "And I tried to put her off, but you know about how well that works." She rolled her eyes, shook her head. Her mom was a force unto herself, and while Kate loved her, of course, sometimes doing battle with her felt like standing in front of an oncoming train and trying to deviate it from its tracks.

A.K.A. it wouldn't work, and she was going to get crushed.

"Doesn't explain Mr. *JaimeTheVet*," Cora pointed out.

Kate knew that. "I just . . . panicked and blurted I was

engaged. My mom got excited. Like *really* excited and I . . . fuck, I couldn't take it back in that moment," she said. "I wanted her to be happy, and I know it's ridiculous because I'm a grown woman, but I just didn't want her to be disappointed in me."

Like they had been when she'd upended her family's lives.

"I don't think your parents could ever be disappointed in you, Katie," Heidi said, pulling her out of the memory. "They brag to my parents all the time, and I swear if I've heard it once, I've heard it a hundred times, 'why can't you be in a normal career like Kate?'" Her tone mimicked her mother's. "'*She* actually sees her family and doesn't spend all her time in the lab—'"

"A lab from which you just quit working," Kate pointed out.

Silence. Eyes going wide.

Then Cora blinked and said, "Nice try, Katie. But we'll stay on the fake engagement topic for the moment." She pointed at Heidi. "*You,* we'll get to later."

Kels lifted her fist for Cora to bump. "This is why we've been friends since elementary school." Her gaze fixed onto Kate's. "So, how long is this fake engagement going to go on?"

Kate winced. "Um . . ."

Kels groaned. "Oh no. Tell me he isn't a jerk."

"No!" She sat up. "No," she repeated. "He's actually really great. I like him so much. He's sweet and good with my family." A smile curved her lips. "He seems determined to take care of me and—"

"Are you paying him?" Kels asked, cold infiltrating her tone.

"She's not," Heidi said. "And I had a full background check run on him. His vet practice is successful, and his family is loaded—even more so than Kate's after her mom's magical aging serum."

Cora tapped her forehead. "The reason I don't have fine lines."

"Background ch—" Kate began.

"Not the point," Kels said to Cora, ignoring Kate. "So, nothing criminal in his background and he's not looking for money. Why is he pretending to be engaged when most guys would run screaming the other direction?"

Three pairs of eyes turned her way, and Kate felt a rush of defensiveness. She wanted to snap out a response.

But, how could she?

She'd thought the same at first, wondered what possible motivation a man like that would want with a woman like her, especially when it came to something as intense and complicated as an engagement, fake or not.

Still, Kate couldn't lie.

That her friends thought that too stung a bit.

"*He*"—Cora gasped, and then they all turned to see Jaime standing in the doorway—"was half in love with Kate from the moment he first saw her smiling in a picture on his friend's feed. *He* spent the last months trying to build a slow communication with her so he wouldn't be a fucking creep who slid into her DMs like he just wanted to get into her pants. *He* tumbled the rest of the way into love with her when he saw how much she loved her family, when he got to see how strongly she cared and took care of those around her. *He* plummeted deeper as he got to know her heart, her humor, her strength." Jaime pushed off the frame, crossed over to her, cupped her cheek lightly. "But he fell deeply, irrevocably in love when she cracked the door enough that she let him take care of her in return."

Her heart was pounding a million miles per hour.

Her lungs seemed to have stopped working.

Her skin prickled, her lips tingled, her fingers had gone numb.

Hell, her *whole* body had gone numb with the exception of where he held her face, the slight roughness of his calloused palm against her skin. "I know it's too soon," he said. "But it's how I feel here." He took her hand, placed it against his chest so she could feel his heart thundering beneath. "And it's how I feel here." He let go, tapped his temple, one half of his mouth curving. "Which is why we're going to have a really long fake engagement. Long enough for you to decide that you want to be engaged to me for real. And then"—his voice dropped—"then I'll get you that diamond Ann was talking about, okay?"

She was mute.

Stunned and warmed through. Pulse still thundering, but her heart open and full to the brim.

He slanted his lips over hers, not skimping on the tongue, not hesitating to tug her close and send her pulse skittering to even higher rates. Then he stepped back, nudged her onto the couch when she wobbled, and brushed the back of his knuckles down her cheek, over her throat. "Now," he said, straightening, his voice pitched to the whole room. "I apologize for intruding on Girl's Night twice in a row. I left my keys to the clinic here last night, and I won't have any staff there early tomorrow to let me in. Will someone lock up behind me?" He unleashed his sexy *JaimeTheVet* smile before turning for the door. "I knocked earlier, but I think you were having too much fun to hear." A glance back. "Or to realize that the last woman in hadn't locked up."

His eyes cut to Kate's, and he winked.

Then he was gone, the sound of the front door closing gunshot loud in the quiet space.

Quiet until they heard a car engine start up.

Quiet until they heard it pull away.

Kate turned dumbfounded eyes to her friends. "Did he say that he loved me?"

Heidi nodded, mute for perhaps the first time in all of the time that Kate had known her.

Cora's head bobbed. "He *did* say it," she murmured. "And

he said it incredibly well." Her stare was glazed, locked on the spot where Jaime had disappeared.

Kels was the first to recover, perhaps because she had her own extremely gorgeous man.

Her own.

Which implied that Kate had *her* own.

And . . . she supposed she did. She'd cracked the door. He'd come in, and he wasn't a jerk or an asshole, hadn't been terrified and run off screaming like his hair was on fire.

He'd stayed.

He'd said . . . God, he'd said so many wonderful things.

"I'm sorry," Kels said, coming over to her. "I made a snap judgment before finding out the facts."

Kate smiled at her friend. "You were just trying to protect me."

"I hurt your feelings." Kels shook her head. "I saw it in your eyes. That wasn't fair of me." She squeezed Kate's knee. "You're my friend, and I love you. I don't want to see you hurt. But that . . ." Another squeeze. "That, honey, is something that only comes around once per life. Don't let it scare you. Grab on to it. Make it yours and hold it tight."

"But it's so soon," she whispered.

"Yeah." Kels stood up and poured Kate another glass of wine. "But sometimes you just know."

"Plus, he seemed inclined on an extended engagement." Cora's lips twitched.

"An extended engagement between the sheets." Heidi grinned, waggled her brows.

They all groaned.

Kels put the drink into Kate's hand, nudged it toward her mouth. "Drink that and keep his words close. You guys have found each other. Now you can take the time to walk the path together."

Heidi frowned. "What path?"

Kels rolled her eyes. "You're hopeless, you know that, right?"

A shrug. "I know that the man just passed his first test."

"True," Cora said when Kels disappeared into the hall, saying she was going to lock the front door. "But also, *I* know that it's now *your* turn on the hot seat. What did Kate mean about you leaving the lab?"

Heidi groaned. "No, I'm not ready. Bug that one"—she nodded at Kate—"some more about the vet. Or what Jaime meant about interrupting a second Girl's Night." Her eyes narrowed. "Are you cheating on us, Katie girl?"

Kate took a sip, smiled sanguinely. "Distractions don't work with us." Another sip. "But because you asked, the first Girl's Night he interrupted was helping me babysit Lacy. He has magical baby skills."

"Hot damn. Walk that path, Katie. Don't deviate," Cora said, clamping her hands over her heart.

Kels came back in and picked up her glass. "Don't get distracted." She turned to Heidi. "Drink that wine and prepare to spill your guts."

Another groan.

But Heidi knew she wasn't going to get off the hook.

She spilled about her job. And after that, Cora complained about her brothers—she had six of them. Yes, six. They were protective and overbearing in a way that almost made Kate's mom seem like a pussy cat. Their dad had died shortly after Cora was born, and they'd made it their personal responsibility to protect Cor from anything and everything that might bring her harm.

And they thought there were a *lot* of things that could bring her harm.

But Cor loved the big lugs, and so the complaining came from a place as much of love as of annoyance.

Sooner or later they needed to realize that Cora was a grown woman with needs, one of which included a need to not be alone for the rest of her life. Oh, and another need, an important one, was hot sex, not that she let her brothers in on *that* sentiment.

Regardless, it was nice to get the heavy out the way then to just sit with her friends and tease and laugh and drink too much as the conversation drifted to reality TV and what they were getting each other for Christmas.

Tradition said they got each other a white elephant gift, along with something they really wanted.

All small things—their budget for both together was forty dollars.

But it made for a fun tradition of getting together on Boxing Day and exchanging gifts.

"Only four more days until presents!" she said with a nod at her tree in the corner of the room several hours later as she shepherded them out the front door.

"Meanie!" Heidi said and stuck her tongue out. "You know I don't have any patience when it comes to surprises."

"Technically, it's only three days since it's after midnight," Kels said, wavering slightly as she made her way into Tanner's arms.

"I stand by my *meanie* statement," Heidi said.

Cora giggled but didn't say anything, just headed down the stairs and for Tanner's car.

Kate smothered a grin and kept walking her friends out. Tanner had knocked on the door after Kelsey had called him not too long before for a ride home—since they were all lightweights and three bottles of wine between them had certainly put them well beyond their limits for operating motor vehicles.

Hell, they could barely operate a doorknob.

A fact that Tanner had busted a gut over after how long it had taken the three of them to figure out the lock and turn the handle.

Three because Kate had eventually nudged her friends to the side and opened the door herself.

She'd always been a little better at holding her alcohol than her friends—something that had been helped even more recently because she and Kelsey had been practicing of late with prickly pear margaritas from their favorite Mexican restaurant.

Anyway, she digressed, but—*shrug*—that was the lovely, pleasant, fuzzy-headed side effect of the booze talking.

Which was probably going to make for a painful morning.

At least for her head.

Her heart, on the other hand, was full. There was champagne in her veins, bubbling and filling her with so much joy that she couldn't wait to see Jaime again.

She'd texted him already, telling him to come back, to come and kiss her goodnight—cough, because she wouldn't mind *more* than a kiss—but it was late, and he hadn't texted back, so he was probably already in bed.

Which made sense. She had the rest of the week off, but he had to work a full day tomorrow—well, later that day—and then another half-day on Christmas Eve. He didn't exactly have the luxury of a midnight-post-Girl's-Night messing around session. Even if she definitely wanted a repeat of the previous evening.

A repeat with the cherry on top. And maybe some chocolate sauce.

And whipped cream.

Mmm.

Just not on her sheets.

Grinning, she checked her cell again, saw that he still hadn't texted back. But that was okay.

He had a life.

Of course, now she wanted that life to be firmly intertwined with hers.

Because, God, what he'd said that night. Unabashedly and without compunction right in front of her friends. Her heart swelled because it meant so freaking much to her and her carefully protected heart. It meant . . . *everything*.

Her eyes burned and she knew she wouldn't be able to resist the urge for one more text before she let sleep take her over.

Just nudging that door open a little wider.

Heidi stumbled, and Kate pushed her sappy thoughts away, focused on getting her goofy ass friends safely into Tanner's car.

"Have fun with the drunk patrol," she said, herding Heidi to his car.

Tanner stopped, glanced from Kelsey to Kate to Cora to Heidi, and though he didn't groan out loud, Kate still saw it cross his face.

"You love me when I'm drunk," Kelsey stage whispered. "It means you're guaranteed to get lucky."

Heidi pretended to gag. "Just drop me off before you start taking his clothes off, okay?"

"No guarantees," Kelsey sing-songed.

Heidi fake gagged again.

At least, Kate *hoped* it was fake.

Tanner was apparently on the same train of thought. "So long as that wasn't a real pretend puke—" He shook his head. "That doesn't make sense. The point is . . . just no puking in the car. Deal?"

"Deal," Cora said and patted his cheek before sitting down and fumbling with her seat belt.

Tanner's eyes rolled to the sky, but he reached over and buckled her in.

"Heidi?" he asked.

"No puking," Heidi said with a nod that made her look like a bobblehead. "Got it."

"I love you, baby!" Kels slurred, leaning heavily against him and throwing her arms around his neck. He stumbled a step, shook his head again, and finished buckling Cora in.

Then he turned to Kelsey and held her close.

Aw.

He rubbed his nose against hers, said, albeit quieter than Kels's blurt, "I love you, too."

Double aw.

Aware she was staring with more than a little jealousy, Kate forced herself to look away.

She snagged Heidi's arm, led her around to the other side of the car, and got her buckled in. "Night, bestie," she said, hugging her quickly. "Thanks for being a good friend."

"Hey!" Cora said, pouting.

Kate sighed then unable to stifle her giggle at the comical appearance of her friend's mock-glower. "Goodnight, other bestie. I love you."

Cora blew her a kiss. "Love you, too."

There was a tap on her shoulder, and Kate sighed again, thinking she was about to declare her third *bestie* of the evening.

Instead, Kels hugged her tight. "Love you."

She squeezed her friend back. "I love *you.*"

A grin and before she could say goodnight, Kelsey gripped her shoulders and stared deeply into her eyes, looking suddenly lucid for all she'd been a slurring, stumbling female just seconds before. "Take the chance, Katie. Leap even though you're terrified."

Kate's heart stuttered. Her throat went tight.

But she found the strength to say, "I think I will, Kels. I think I *have* to."

A confident smile from her friend.

"Yes, babe. You do."

"Not to break up the tender moment," Tanner said gently, though his eyes were soft. "But I'd better get Goofy and Goofier home while my seats are still safe."

Kate snorted and stepped back so he could urge Kels into the seat, buckle the belt. "Good luck with that," she teased. "But I think your race against the clock is going to be getting Kels home before she falls asleep."

"Good thing I like her unconscious," he teased.

Another snort, this time paired with Kelsey's outraged gasp. Of course, her outrage was diminished by the amusement dancing across her eyes. "I promise I won't fall asleep *this* time."

"Yeah, yeah," Tanner grumbled. "I've heard it all before."

But his gaze was warm, and he wrapped his jacket around Kels before carefully shutting the door. Then he turned to Kate, met her stare, and said, "For the record, I second her statement." He brushed his fingers over her jaw and pressed a kiss to her forehead. "Do it, Kate. Leap and trust that he'll catch you."

"You haven't met him," she whispered.

"But Kels has," he said. "And she's the smartest person I've ever met." He stepped back, glanced through the window, and smiled ruefully at his woman who was already passed out asleep in the passenger's seat. "I'd bet on her logic, any day of the week."

Kate just nodded.

Because she agreed with him.

Kelsey's logic. Heidi's fire and spunk. Cora's sweet steadfastness.

And her.

Her giving. Her taking. Her caring. Her . . . love for the man who'd bared his heart, who'd shown up for her when she needed, and who'd lain the groundwork for a trust they could continue to build over time.

She waved as Tanner drove away.

Then she threw the door wide open.

Forget inches.

She was dealing in feet.

NINETEEN

Jaime

THIS WAS PROBABLY A MISTAKE.

But . . . she'd texted him that her friends had left, that she wanted him to come over, and though he'd already been in bed, Jaime found that sleep wouldn't pull him under.

Not when his woman wanted him.

His. Woman.

The last time he'd thought that had been during his days with Lori the previous year, but even then, the days, the time he'd spent with his ex, had never been like this.

His mom used to tell his sisters, *"You have to date a few bad ones in order to find the right one."* He'd always thought that was ridiculous. Normal people met each other, dated, stayed together, or moved on.

But then he'd dated a bad one.

He'd dated Lori.

And he'd understood exactly what his mom had meant.

Ultimately, it was a good thing. He didn't think he would have had the strength to say what he had that night, to keep moving forward when he'd overheard the conversation, to declare himself in front of a room of women who were prepared to dislike him.

Except . . . Kate.

She clearly loved her friends. They clearly loved her.

It was a simple as that.

So, it was nothing for him to give her what she needed. Now, he hoped she'd take the words, the sentiment, and hold it close.

Hence, him being on her doorstep.

She'd texted. He'd come.

But now it was almost one in the morning. The house was dark, except for the bright white lights of her Christmas tree in the family room.

And he was looming on her porch like a burglar in the middle of the night.

He'd texted and waited in his car.

Had texted again before going onto the porch and trying the handle, wanting to make sure she'd locked up behind herself, if she was, in fact, sleeping.

She had.

But now he'd driven over here and was finding it very hard to leave.

He wanted to hold her, to kiss her, to make sure she wasn't going to retreat—

The door opened, revealing legs in fuzzy striped pajama pants, her breasts barely contained in a pale blue top with dangerously thin straps, and Kate looking up at him with sleepy eyes and a warm smile.

"I didn't hear my phone," she murmured.

Jaime ran a finger down one of those thin straps. "Want me to go and let you sleep?"

A shake of her head.

Then she stepped forward and into his arms. "I love you."

The impact of her words was visceral. A sheer punch to the gut that had him sucking in a breath and fighting against the urge to drag her closer, to slant his mouth across hers, to kiss her with every ounce of joy those words brought.

But then she kept talking. "It terrifies me, but I do, baby. I do love you. But . . . I don't know if I'm *ready* to." She shook her head, stepped back. "I know that doesn't make the least bit of sense. How can I love you but not be ready? Because I feel it so strongly here"—she thumped a fist on her chest, over her heart —"but I'm terrified that I'm going to get caught in a maelstrom, that I'm going to let it in, and then I'll be lost, blown to the four corners of the world and not able to find my way back."

God, he loved this woman.

If he'd thought it had taken courage to tell her friends what he was feeling, this was so much more.

This was the depth of her vulnerability laid bare.

He threaded his hand in her hair, stepped close enough that her body was pressed to his, front to front. "I can't take away your fear."

She blinked, lips parting. "Wh-what?"

"I can't make you not afraid, Red."

Her breath shuddered out. "I-I—"

"I love you," he said, nudging her inside and closing the door behind them since it was cold. He kept hold of her as he leaned back against the wooden panel. "I've never felt this way for a woman, but I also know it's been a week. I can get a stubborn dog to take a pill. I can calculate the dosage of carprofen for an eighty-pound German Shepherd. I can start an IV on a pissed-off cat, but I can't take away your fear." He rested his forehead against hers. "God, I want to, baby. I want to make everything all right, heal that giant heart of yours, and ride off into the sunset." He pressed his cheek to her temple, held her tight. "But this is real life, so all I can give you is time and my love and the tools for us to ascend that fucking mountain and make it over to the other side together."

She shuddered, and he felt a hot tear leak out of the corner of her eye, drip down her jaw. "Together?"

Fingers in the silk of her hair, mouth next to her ear, bodies close. "Yeah, Red. Together."

Silence.

Her throat working.

Another hot tear.

Then a halting chuckle. "Damn, baby," she said. "It would be so much easier if you could just make all the bad stuff go away." A breath. "I want to make it to the other side of that rainbow."

He leaned back, stared into those pretty whiskey eyes. "I'll pick up some armor. Maybe a white horse."

She sniffed then smiled before rising on tiptoe to press a quick kiss to his lips. "Me, too."

Give. Take.

Fuck, he loved this woman.

His ALARM CAME FAR TOO SOON, but Jaime couldn't complain about waking up with Kate draped all over him.

The world's best blanket, that was for sure.

A grumpy blanket, who groaned when his alarm blared. He quickly shut it off and slipped from the bed, tugging on the clothes that he'd worn the night before. They'd ended up crumpled on the floor after Kate had taken his hand and dragged him to her bedroom.

Then had her wicked way with him.

Not that he was complaining.

Having a sexy, turned-on Kate below him, hips moving, breasts bare, head thrown back as she came around him was no hardship.

It was a hard *something*.

Snorting, he knelt on the mattress and kissed the base of her spine. She was still naked, neither of them having bothered with pajamas several hours before. He'd just blearily made sure his alarm was good to go then gathered her close and let sleep overtake him.

Now, he tugged the sheets up and over her and disappeared into her bathroom, waiting until the door was closed before turning on the lights. He didn't want to wake her; knew she had the day off. Blinking against the brightness, he remembered she'd drowsily mentioned an extra toothbrush under the sink, and he located it before brushing his teeth and splashing some water on his face.

Feeling slightly more human, he turned out the lights, waited for his eyes to adjust, then cracked the door, tiptoeing quietly into Kate's bedroom.

But she was sitting up, sheet held to her chest, hair a fucking mess that he itched to run his fingers through. He crossed over to her, sat on the bed, and lightly kissed her mouth. "I'm sorry," he said. "Did I wake you?"

Her forehead dropped to his shoulder. "No."

"You okay?"

A nod.

He nudged her down. "Go back to sleep, Red. I'll see you tonight."

"But—" She yawned, started to sit up. "I should make you breakfast."

He nudged her back down. "Another time. Sleep, love."

"I—"

Jaime tucked the covers tightly around her. "There. You're

trapped." He brushed her hair back, kissed her forehead. "Raincheck on breakfast."

Her eyes closed.

He smiled. So fucking beautiful.

He pushed to his feet and started for the door.

"Jaime—"

And stubborn. He sighed. "No, breakfast, Red."

Another yawn, a hint of tart in her tone. "I was just going to say, there's a key in the drawer by the oven."

Even a little cranky and tired, she undid him.

"I love you."

"I lo . . ." Sleep pulled her under, the rest of the words a mumble.

But that was okay because he felt them in his heart anyway.

Jaime slipped from the room, headed downstairs, and out to his car. But he damned sure made certain to stop by the kitchen and grab the key from the drawer before he left.

No more closed doors.

He had the key.

TWENTY

Kate

BY THE TIME she woke up fully after Jaime left, the sun was bright enough in the sky to rival her high school sleeping in days.

And her head . . . well, it felt a little like high school, too.

Alcohol and sex and not knowing her limits.

Except, she kind of knew her limits when it came to Jaime. That being, she had *no* limits when it came to the lovely, sexy man who'd barreled through the door to her heart and made himself right at home.

Then again, she'd thrown the door wide open.

"That's right," she said, stretching long and slow but keeping her eyes closed because the sun was ouchie.

Technical term, that.

Snorting, but still feeling very satisfied with herself, she rolled over, peeked enough to grab her cell, and slit open one eye to type out a message to Jaime.

You know, I was thinking this whole thing was my fault.

She pulled the covers over her head, checked her emails while she waited, but she'd barely gotten her inbox opened when her phone buzzed.

Oh, it's definitely your fault.

Kate chuckled.

I was referring to the fact that you're stuck with me now, rather than the fake engagement.

A pause.

I was, too.

She laughed outright that time, feeling warm and fuzzy inside and just . . . so much in love.

Barry is here for his check-up, so I need to go. Enjoy your day off.

My heart! Squee! Also, I'll let you go take care of that cock.

Kate (and in case you couldn't tell, that was a warning because I can't get a boner at work).

She giggled.

See you tonight? *angel emoji*

Wild horses couldn't keep me away.

*And you've taken care of wild horses—or regular ones
anyway, so I know you mean it. *horse emoji, heart eyes
emoji, celebration emoji, heart emoji**

**kissing emoji* Proof that I've kept up my studying. See
you tonight, Red.*

Kate didn't reply, other than with a heart to keep giving *him*
more proof that her emoji skills were as strong as ever before
setting her phone on her nightstand and pulling the covers back
up and over her.

Happy.

She was happy and fulfilled and . . . she didn't have a
Christmas present for him!

How did she not have a Christmas present?

It was two days away. They would be sitting with her family
at her parents' house with presents all around, and she hadn't
bought him anything.

Of course, a week ago she hadn't thought she'd needed to do
any more buying.

But . . . he meant a lot, had done more to transform her life,
her heart in less time than any other person she had ever met.

And he deserved a present.

A *good* present.

Because he'd given her the gift of time, of courage, of
cracking open the door to her heart.

"Well, you can't just get him a door, Kate," she muttered,
throwing back the covers and blinking against the bright before
she got out of bed. Shower. Clothes. Present. Dinner. That was
her plan.

She'd feed him, coax him into staying the night.

And in the morning, she'd make him breakfast then see him
off to work properly.

Perhaps with a blow job.

Talk about presents.

"You're a dork, Kate McLeod," she said to herself as she walked into the bathroom and turned on the shower.

Hot water paired with shampoo and conditioner went a long way to shaking off her hangover. It did not, however, help her figure out what to get Jaime for Christmas. Because what did one get their fake fiancé, their lover, the man they wanted to build something serious and long-term with . . . that they'd only known a week?

A book, maybe, she considered as she blow-dried her hair.

Or perhaps a T-shirt? He looked really good in T-shirts. Except that wasn't really personal now, was it?

She wanted something thoughtful, something perfect for this man she was just starting to know, but this man she also already knew down into the deepest parts of his heart.

Jaime was . . . well, he wasn't perfect, but she thought that he was perfect for her.

She wanted her gift to show that.

To be the beginning of—

"You're making this too big, you dope," she muttered to herself, shutting off the blow dryer and staring at herself in the mirror. Shining red hair, so bright she used to hate the garish color. Over the years she'd grown to appreciate it somewhat, just as she felt deep down that she could grow to appreciate herself.

To not shut people out and blame it on them.

To be strong enough to be open.

No more asshole superpowers. Her new one was going to be . . .

Brown eyes stared back at her, question in the depths.

Then she smiled and picked up her tube of moisturizer.

"Being happy is going to be my superpower," she promised. "To stop being such a weakling and grab on to my happy."

Nodding, she slapped on some makeup, slipped into a festive sweater and boots, a scarf, and her cozy jacket. A cup of coffee and a piece of toast later, and she was prepped to brave the last-minute Christmas shopping crowds.

Confident. Strong. Excited.

Little did she know what awaited her at the mall was going to shatter all of that.

SHE'D GONE from searching for the perfect gift for Jaime that would express exactly what she was feeling in her heart to just wanting to find *any* gift.

Everything was cleared out.

Crumbs.

Proverbial, that was. All she had were proverbial crumbs. Oh, and a tabletop ping pong set.

Somehow that didn't scream true love.

Sighing, she set the box down and knew she was back to the drawing board. She was probably being too picky, should just snap up some lingerie and wrap herself up as Jaime's present.

Except, how was he going to open *that* present with her family on Christmas?

They did a small exchange before the neighborhood started traipsing through. Her family would expect her to have gotten Jaime something, and she didn't even want to attempt a conversation with her brother and dad that insinuated Jaime had already gotten his present earlier.

Bow-chicka-bow-wow.

Nope. No, thank you. She liked all of Jaime's body parts exactly where they were.

Of course, she could always get him lingerie *and* something else.

A slow smile curved her lips as she walked out of the entrance to the shop. The kiosk in front of her sold bands for smart watches, but one in particular caught her eye, and she knew it would be perfect for him to open in front of her family.

Then she went to the ridiculously expensive lingerie store and spent far too much money on lace. Red, because it was his favorite color.

It was as she was walking out of the store, carrying an extra bag filled with emerald green lace that she hadn't been able to pass up—she had to stick with the festive season and get outfits in both holiday colors, right?—when she saw it.

Or rather, *him*.

Jaime.

With his arm around a beautiful redhead. She was snuggled close, gazing adoringly up at him.

Her heart turned to ice.

Was he—?

No. He couldn't. He wasn't an asshole. He was kind and patient and . . . she'd only known him a week. And he had his hands on another woman when he'd promised to build something rock-solid between them, a trust that would never falter.

He brushed back a strand of the redhead's hair, tucked it behind her ear.

Bile burned the back of Kate's throat. She knew what it felt like for him to do that, to touch *her* that way . . . and he was doing it to another woman.

Her heart cracked.

She wanted to run to her car, to lock herself away, to slam the door shut.

But she forced herself to take a breath. To think this through.

There must be an explanation. She couldn't have opened her heart and been so wrong about the man. She *couldn't have*.

Shaking legs carrying her over to a bench, she pulled out her phone and called him.

Then watched as he glanced down at his watch and declined the call.

Another crack. Another fissure.

Still, she needed to try once more. She didn't need to be one of those idiot females who made a snap judgment then ran off when there was a perfectly reasonable explanation.

No matter how much that explanation might hurt.

She typed out a text.

Are you free for lunch? I'm finally coherent.

He glanced down at his watch again. Kate nibbled at her lip. But then he said something to the redhead, stepped away, and reached into his pocket. A second later, he had his cell in hand and was typing.

She held her breath, waited for it to ping through onto her phone.

Ten seconds passed then her cell buzzed.

Can't. Sorry. I'm slammed at the clinic.

Reading those words snatched away the breath she'd been holding, had the door in her heart slamming shut as hurt overwhelmed her.

"Fuck," she whispered, rubbing her hand over her chest, over the spot where her heart was breaking into pieces. She shoved her phone into her purse, picked up her bags, and took a step toward the couple, preparing to unleash her fury.

Then . . . she stopped, the crowd of shoppers all around her.

And she couldn't.

God, why *couldn't* she?

Maybe it was the kiss to the top of the woman's hand. Maybe it was the way she pointed and smiled coyly at the lingerie shop that Kate had spent an exorbitant amount of money in just minutes before.

Maybe it was the sinking, oppressive, really *fucking* sad feeling.

Maybe it was just her realization that for all her pretending, she'd been right about her superpower all along.

Assholes.

They cropped up everywhere.

Even when she least suspected.

TWENTY-ONE

Jaime

HE STOWED the bags in the back of his car and got in, his sister, Tammy, already in the front seat of his car.

She'd come into town unexpectantly and had tagged along on his Christmas shopping expedition for Kate, teasing him relentlessly for his last-minute mission. Until she'd seen the store he wanted to get the big present from.

"I'm going to marry her," he'd announced.

Then her eyes had widened, but she'd quickly shrugged off her shock and helped him make his selection.

Gleefully spending his money.

But that was okay. He was happy to see his favorite sis, even if it was just on a pit stop before she headed to their parents' house.

"Still can't believe you're making me go home alone," she grumbled as he navigated the crazy parking and pedestrian situation at the mall.

"Unfortunately," he said. "The clinic will be open the day after, and I need to make sure I'm there."

It was the truth, but also not.

Because while the clinic *was* open. It hadn't been until a week ago when he'd told the front desk to open up the schedule for a few hours in the afternoon.

He'd kept the staff off, and no one had actually booked the appointments.

But his family didn't need to know that.

The truth was that he didn't want to be away from Kate. Not this soon. Not when they were just starting out. And it wasn't like he could bring her home. His family didn't even know he was fake engaged, let alone seeing a woman.

Though, he knew both of those—minus the fake part— would change as soon as Tammy spilled the beans.

Fine with him.

He wanted to be with Kate, no holds barred.

The sooner everyone on the planet knew that fact, the better.

And so, maybe he was feeling the tiniest bit possessive.

Meh. A man had to do what he had to do, and that included making it clear to the rest of the populace that Kate was his.

"Hmm."

"What?" he asked, playing innocent, even as he turned in the direction of the airport. Tammy needed to get to her flight, and he needed to get back to the clinic. He'd already pushed several appointments when she'd shown up unexpectantly. He didn't want to disappoint his clients, knew their time was just as important.

"And none of this staying here for the holiday has anything to do with this Kate?"

"Not going to say it's not a benefit," he muttered. "Sex with the woman I love versus opening a poop brown sweater from Aunt Janet."

Tammy smacked him. "You're terrible." A beat. "But not wrong." Sighing, she leaned back in her seat. "I miss sex."

He groaned. "No, my ears!"

"What? You can talk about it, but I can't?"

"Yes," he said, flashing her a grin. "Exactly that. You're my baby sister. That means I'm going to go through the rest of my life pretending you've never had sex."

"Newsflash, dumbass," she grumbled. "I've had sex. Loads and loads of really hot, really awesome—"

"La. La. La."

"Don't cover your ears," she said. "You need your hands to drive."

He laughed, shook his head. "Wasn't planning on it." Jaime paused, checking traffic as he merged onto the freeway. "It didn't work out with your guy?"

"No."

"Want to talk about it?"

He saw her make a face out of the corner of his eye, expected the change in conversation that came a second later. "When do I get to meet this Kate?"

"When I can get her to not run screaming from our family," he said dryly.

"Good luck with that." But it was a lighthearted response, one equal to his words. Because Kate would love his family. It was the same reason he'd felt so comfortable stepping into hers. Love and teasing. Jokes and banter around a dinner table. Enjoying each other's company. Not hesitating to drop anything to help, to be there, to show they cared.

Two sides of the same coin.

He just had an extra sibling in the mix.

Which is why he knew he'd be making a trip home soon—as much as he grumbled, he loved his family, would miss seeing them for the holiday. He just hoped that he could convince Kate to keep trusting him enough to hop on a plane with him.

Tammy changed the topic to work, and they spent the remainder of the ride to the airport talking about her plans for her job.

She was considering a move to the Bay Area but wasn't sure she wanted to get mixed up in tech, not when her skills in Human Resources meant she could work in a variety of fields.

"Well, just remember that your favorite brother is here," he said, hugging her tight.

"My favorite *older* brother," she teased. "My favorite younger brother has decided his role is jet-setting around the world and giving our mother coronaries." They shared a grin, knowing that wasn't hard to do. Their mom wasn't exactly known as being easy-going.

"He's good at that," Jaime said.

"*Damned* good."

"We should take notes."

She laughed and rose on tiptoe, pressing a kiss to his cheek. "Love you, Jaime-Maimy."

He groaned. "Really? Pulling out old nicknames?"

Tammy grabbed her bag. "It's part of my privilege as a younger sister."

"Safe flight, Tammy Two Shoes."

A roll of her eyes. "And yours, too, apparently. I always hated that nickname."

He tugged her ponytail. "At least you've figured out you only need one shoe on each foot now."

"They were slippers!" She tossed up her hands. "I was four. How was I supposed to know that you didn't wear hard shoes over them?"

"I'm not touching that," he said with a smirk.

"Good. Don't. Love you."

"Love you, too."

Then after one more and a wave at the automatic doors, she was inside the terminal and Jaime was back in his car, driving to the clinic.

The rest of the afternoon passed in a blur, an emergency pushing his already messed up schedule into the realm of fucked. He kept his head down, tried to stay focused, but as the hours passed, a knot grew in his stomach.

At first, he thought it was something he was missing with the dog.

It had been hit by a car, had suffered some severe injuries.

But as time went on, as he stabilized the lab mix, he realized it wasn't the case or the clinic, or the devastated owner.

This was about Kate.

She hadn't texted back earlier.

And when he sent her a message, saying he was caught at the clinic, would still be several hours, she didn't respond to that one either.

Nor did she pick up his call when he got out of surgery and washed up, having finished up with his other clients and sent his techs home.

It was just him and Roger, the lab mix, whose prognosis was good, but who was loopy and needed more fluids before his owner could come and take him home. Pushing the sinking feeling away, he called his client, told her the good news.

Then he called Kate again.

And again, she didn't answer.

The knot in his stomach grew, and his fingers flew across the keyboard. He had the distinct notion that the woman he loved was slipping away, and he didn't know why . . . or how to keep her.

Don't close the door, Red.

No response.

"Fuck," he muttered, closing his eyes, and sliding down the wall.

Roger's tail thumped once on the floor.

"Good boy," he said gently.

He sat and waited, and as each minute passed without a reply from Kate, his heart sank further.

He was losing her, and he had no clue how to stop it.

TWENTY-TWO

Kate

SHE HADN'T CRIED, knew that would come later.

For now, she wrapped Jaime's presents and shoved them under the tree.

Maybe she'd burn them later.

All that lace would make for a nice flame.

For now, she was digging a giant hole in the back yard. The front was pretty much set, and it wasn't like she could add any more bulbs than she already had. It was December and too cold to plant much else.

Maybe she'd buy a huge tree.

Then bury the ashes of her lingerie in it.

"Fucking asshole men," she muttered, still digging. Her T-shirt soaked with sweat, though it was barely above forty—and that was cold for California, okay? She was in old, baggy jeans, had dirt covering her hands and arms, and she suspected, her cheeks. But she didn't stop digging, not even when the sun went down and it got colder, the impact of the shovel stinging her palms. "Fucking. Asshole. Cheating. Asshole. Fucking. Asshole.

Men," she said, the metal blade reverberating through the ground with each grunted-out word.

"It might take you a while to dig that hole big enough if you're trying to bury my body."

Silken male words.

And she was pissed, but not pissed enough to miss the caution underlying the attempt at a joke.

Well, no. Charming wasn't going to work with her. Nope. No fucking way.

She turned back to her hole and kept digging.

Soft footsteps. "Did you not see my call? My texts?"

Oh, she'd seen them. Meaningless words from a fucking cheating asshole. God, remembering how it felt to see him lie to her from fifty feet away, seeing him dismiss her so easily, it made her already broken heart hurt even more.

But she wasn't a weakling.

She stabbed the shovel into the dirt and spun to face him.

"How was the mall?" she snapped, crossing her arms and glaring up at him.

Clarity on his face, silence falling. But he didn't deny he'd been there, with that woman. "It's not what you think."

Damn. Dammit all to hell.

The idiotic part of her that had been holding on to some random slice of hope—that he had an identical twin who was dating a gorgeous redhead, or something equally ridiculous—shriveled up and died.

She turned, returned to digging her hole.

Maybe she *would* make it big enough to bury him.

"Go home, Jaime."

"No."

Fury tore through her, and she whipped around to face him. "You're just like all the rest of them. I trusted you," she shouted.

"I let you in, let you see parts of me that no one else has ever been able to, and y-you—"

Eyes burning, she spun back to the hole.

"Kate."

"No!" She scooped up a pile of dirt and threw it at him.

It landed with a soft smack against his chest, turning his white T-shirt black in the harsh glow of the floodlights she had shining.

"You're a liar!" she screamed.

"Yes," he said.

Fucking asshole. *Fucking* asshole. Kate shook her head and got back to her hole. But just when the tip of the shovel made contact with the dirt, it was pulled from her hand and tossed aside.

"I *was* at the mall," he said, tugging her against his chest. The smell of the damp earth filled her nose.

"I know." She shoved, tried to wriggle out of his hold.

He held fast. "With my sister."

"I kn—"

Her words died on her lips.

"With your sister?" she asked numbly, her fury turning to horror to embarrassment to fear. Because this would make him change his mind.

"Yes, Red."

She'd given him a glimpse of the terrified woman inside and—

A hand on her jaw, tilting her head back, forcing her eyes to his. "Stop."

"I—"

He kissed her.

The soil—okay, it was really mud—squished between their chests, a cold shock sinking into her skin even as his mouth scorched her to the bone.

He pulled back. "I shouldn't have lied." He rested his fore-head to hers. "My sister, Tammy, showed up unexpectedly, and I took advantage of her to help me buy your gift."

"Jaime—"

"I lied," he said. "I promised to build trust, and I didn't do that."

"No," she said, gripping his arms. "I was there buying your gift, and I saw you with her, and . . . I didn't trust you." Shame washed over her. "I acted like an idiot, calling and texting instead of just walking up to you and finding out the truth."

"Patience."

"I know." She blinked. "I didn't have any. I'm sorry. I should have—"

"No, Red. I meant you need to have patience with yourself." She froze. "You're not mad?"

"That you're digging the hole you want to bury my body in?" He rubbed his nose against hers. "No, baby. Fuck, I don't know what I would have done if I was in the same boat as you. Freaked out? Beat the asshole up? Kissed you in front of everyone and make it clear you were mine?"

She bit her lip. "I should have gone for the last."

He nodded. "Yeah, that's what I would have voted for, too."

"I don't want to have a hard time trusting you," she said, voice shaking. "I love you and want to not doubt us together, to not doubt *you*—"

"But we've been fake-engaged for a week," he said. "Cut yourself some slack."

Kate nodded and knew that it was time for her to tell him the last piece of the puzzle, something even Heidi didn't know.

The real reason it was so hard for her to trust anyone.

"I didn't use to be like this."

He stilled, pale brown eyes on hers. She shivered.

"Hold on, honey," he said gently, and then he bent, picked

her up into his arms, and carried her into her house, bypassing the kitchen, the family room, moving up the stairs, and passed the bedroom.

He carried her all the way into the bathroom then turned on the shower.

It wasn't until steam filled the space that she realized she was chilled to the bone and trembling.

Her shoes hit the floor. Her clothes joined them.

Jaime's followed suit.

Then he was lifting her into his arms again, stepping into the shower stall, hot water sluicing over her, warming her, combining with his tight hold and stopping her shivers.

Only then did he say, "Tell me."

Her eyes dropped to the tile and she sighed. "It's stupid when I think of what started it."

"I don't care how stupid it is," he said. "I just want to know what hurt you." Fingers on her cheek. "Take away the power. Let the pain be washed away."

"It's not fair that you're so normal and I'm—"

"Wonderful, smart, sexy, loveable Kate."

She sniffed, released a ragged breath. And then she told him the reason her family had to move when she was in high school.

Why she'd gone away to college. Why it had been damned hard for Heidi to break through her tough shell, and her friend had only been successful because Heidi rivaled Kate in her stubbornness.

"I was bullied," she admitted.

Surprise across his eyes and his jaw clenched. "Oh, Red."

She shrugged. "At first, it was just normal kids' stuff. A jerky boy who made fun of my hair, a mean girl who teased me for my freckles. God, this is *so* embarrassing." She covered her face with her hands. "It's so long ago—"

One move had her pressed to the tile.

She gasped at the cold tile on her back, contrasted against the hot body pressed to her front.

"Not stupid." Terse words. *"Tell me."*

Kate swallowed hard, knew that she would have an argument on her hands if she denied him. And . . . he was right. Wasn't it beyond time for her to stop letting this have power over her?

"Middle school came," she said. "I developed early." And embarrassment gave way to anger, because what was done to her wasn't right. It wasn't stupid kid stuff any longer. It was mean and hurtful and . . . illegal. "I had this crush on a boy. I thought he was the cutest. Long hair"—a smile in his direction—"gorgeous blue eyes, and he was two whole years older. An eighth-grader when I was a lowly sixth-grader."

Her fingers tightened on his shoulders when the memory cropped up, and she went to release them, not wanting to hurt Jaime.

"Don't," he said. "Hold on as tight as you need, Red."

God, she loved this man.

But she wanted to finish this, to be done with the painful chapter, to do that looking forward she'd promised herself earlier.

"His sister was in my grade. We'd been friends for years, but grew apart in middle school, and it went as you might expect." Kate sighed. "She started hanging with a different group, with the popular kids, and when they found out I liked him, they took pictures of me changing."

Now Jaime's grip tightened.

"Not naked," she said. "But close enough. I was in a bra and underwear, changing from P.E., and those pictures were *everywhere.* The sole good thing about this is it was before Facebook and Snapchat and Instagram. But they printed out the pictures and taped them up all over school. I'd tear one down and then

I'd open my locker and another copy would be there. Or go to the bathroom and there was one taped to the stall door, and to the mirror, and passed out at football games." She shuddered out a breath. "*Everyone* saw them. It was . . . well, for a girl not comfortable in her own skin, especially for one with boobs and curves that were more developed, it was horrible." A shiver had Jaime turning up the heat on the shower, and she was grateful. "Then they spread the rumor that I'd known about the camera, that I was posing for the pictures, and . . . guys made assumptions. Hell, girls and teachers did, too."

Her chin dropped to her chest.

"Red," he said hoarsely. "I'm sorry."

"That's not all," she whispered then forced herself to lift her head, to strengthen her tone. "The police opened an investigation, and because I was underage and the pictures were shared, it was considered child pornography."

"Shit."

"Yeah." She stroked her hands down his arms. "It was the right thing to do, obviously, but . . ."

"It blew back harder on you."

Kate nodded. "Yeah," she said. "Eventually, we moved. The timing was good in a way. My mom had made the sale, was ready for a new job, and my dad could work remotely. But Ann and Jake were devastated." She leaned her head back against the tile. "They had a hard time adjusting to the new school, to leaving their friends, their sports teams. I think they understood as we got older, but I knew they resented it at the time."

"Your parents did the right thing."

"I know," she said. "I just hate that they had to, hate that even after the move I wasn't even in any shape to go to school in-person. I home-schooled until I left for college."

"You were violated, Kate. People don't just bounce back to normal."

She sighed. "I know."

"Do you?" he asked quietly.

Her normal response would be to say *of course* she knew. But if the last week had taught her anything, it was that her first instinct wasn't necessarily right.

"I'm working on it," she admitted. "I think I spent so long trying to shove everything down and move forward like nothing was wrong that I didn't realize exactly how much it had affected me, even now. Silly, huh?"

He shook his head, held her tighter. "No, Red. That's normal."

"Oh yeah?" she said, wanting to turn the page on this, to grasp on to something lighter, something not so painful.

Not that she was going to ignore it or pretend it had never happened.

Not any longer.

She was just going to put it behind her. To—in Jaime's words—take away its power, wash it down the drain.

"Yes," he agreed, pressing a kiss to her cheek, to the tip of her nose, to her forehead. "Completely, totally normal."

"Well, what's your quote-unquote normal that still haunts you?"

He didn't hesitate, just offered himself up on a platter. "I wet the bed until I was eight or nine. Sometimes I still wake up in terror, thinking I've done it again, and it's been more than twenty years."

"Oh, baby," she murmured.

"Pathetic, right?"

"No." She kissed him.

"Not gonna tease me about Pull-Ups or a mattress protector?" he asked and though his tone was light, she picked up on the nearly hidden vein of embarrassment of a painful memory.

He'd given.

He'd given so much.

So, it took no effort at all to tell him the truth. "No, baby," she said. "Not that. *Never* that."

His eyes softened, and he held her tight for another long moment.

Then he leaned back, propped her back under the stream of water. "Should we finish getting cleaned up and then go back to digging your hole?"

Her lips tipped up. "That's an oxymoron if I've ever heard one."

A chuckle, hands pouring soap onto her loofa. "Well, then, we're both wet and naked, whatever shall we do?"

She burst out laughing. He joined in.

Then she snagged the loofa. "I've got some plans."

Oh boy, did she have some plans.

TWENTY-THREE

Jaime

IT WAS CHRISTMAS DAY. Well, Christmas *evening*, and Jaime was staring in shock at the crowd of people in the hallway of Kate's parents' house. "What are you guys—" A shake of his head. "*How* are you guys here?"

Tammy pushed past his parents and walked up to him. "I called Mom from the airport, told them about the girl, about your Kate and how you bought"—

This was the point he started making slicing motions with his hands.

Of course, his sister missed them.

"—her a big, fat diamond—"

More slicing motions. More ignoring.

"—and were going to ask her to marry you—"

For fuck's sake. Half the crowd might already think he'd popped the question, but Jaime had plans. Plans he should have enacted that morning, but she'd distracted him with gorgeous red lace.

Then with green lace.

And . . . time had gotten away from them. So much that they'd barely made it to the party on time.

For Christ's sake, they hadn't even cleared the hallway before the knock had come.

"How did you—?" He blinked. "I mean." He shook his head. "You've never been here before."

Tammy held up her phone. "Find Your Phone family plan works both ways, buckaroo." A grin. "We tailed your car."

"And then barged into a house you didn't know?" he asked.

He loved his family, but . . . for fuck's sake. Were they trying to nuke his personal life?

"Hi," Kate said, extending her hand to his sister.

Jaime sighed. "The wannabe spy is Tammy, my sister. My mom and dad—" He pointed to his parents, but Kate had slipped by him, closed the distance.

"I'm Kate," she said to his mom. "It's so nice to finally meet you, Mr. and Mrs. Huntington."

"Tawny, please. And this is my husband, Andrew."

"So nice to officially meet you both," Kate said. "Jaime talks about you all the time—"

"What's this?"

The crowd turned to see Marabelle in the hall, her hair perfectly coiffed, a reindeer-printed apron wrapped around her slender frame.

Silence then, "Mom! Isn't this great?" Kate said. "Jaime's family came to town and surprised him."

To her credit, Marabelle didn't miss a beat.

She walked over, introduced herself to Jaime's parents, then they completed the introductions with Jaime's other sister, Penny, and his brother, Brad.

"Mom," he said, tugging her a little ways away and sending death glares at his siblings for letting his mom bundle them all into the car and drive out. Not one of them appeared unabashed. Hell, they were all so nosy, they'd probably encouraged her. "Not that I'm not happy to see you," he said quietly, "but . . ."

She lifted her chin. "You were too busy to come home, so we decided to come out and meet this girl," his mother finished for him. "Do you know how expensive last-minute flights are? We ended up driving out."

"From Utah?" Kate's mom exclaimed, tuning into the conversation. "Gosh, you guys must be so tired. Please, come in. Dinner's almost ready."

"Oh, we wouldn't want to intrude," his mom said.

Jaime snorted.

And got a smack on the back of the head for his trouble.

But Marabelle ignored them both. Instead, she took his mom's arm and led her down the hall. "There's always plenty of food. We'll just bring in some more chairs. Harry! Dave! Jake! I need chairs."

"We'll help," Brad said, snagging Penny and Tammy and hauling them down the hall after the moms.

Hell.

The moms.

"Welcome to the family, Kate," his dad said. A shake of his head. "For the record, I tried to stop them."

Kate giggled.

And Jaime? He decided to roll with it. What choice did he have otherwise? "At least we won't get sweaters from Aunt Janet this year," he said hopefully.

"Oh no." His father patted his shoulder. "Your mother packed those."

Kate giggled again, and with another shake of his head, Jaime's dad followed everyone else down the hall.

"They drove out?" she whispered, wide eyes meeting his.

Jaime rubbed his suddenly throbbing temple. "Apparently."

Kate turned, wrapped her arms around him. "They love you."

"I circle back to my original statement," he muttered, "and repeat *apparently*."

Warm whiskey eyes slid up to his. "I think we need to come clean about the engagement."

"Why?"

She frowned. "Jaime, I don't want to lie anymore."

"Neither do I." He stepped back.

"Exactly," she murmured, turning for the kitchen. "So, I'll just go in there and let everyone know—"

He snagged her hand, tugged her back to face him.

"Wh—?" She began, brows drawn together.

Probably because he wasn't on his feet any longer.

Instead, he'd sunk down onto one knee.

"Jaime."

He reached into the jacket he hadn't even had a chance to take off yet and pulled out the ring he'd bought with Tammy. More plans gone askew—he'd thought to sneak Kate out back, to snag a quiet moment and make her truly his.

Instead . . . family.

Instead . . . give and take.

Instead . . . he found he didn't give a shit if it was the perfect moment. He just wanted this woman in his life.

Forever.

"I didn't ask you to marry me properly the first time," he murmured and opened the box. "Will you make me the happiest man on the planet and marry me, Kate McLeod?"

"After a *long* engagement," her dad muttered.

Kate jumped, he blinked, and they both turned, saw that both of their families had crowded into the hall. She sighed and shook her head, a slow smile curving that luscious mouth before she dropped down next to him, leaned close, and whispered in his ear, "If I say, yes, will you grow your hair back and share all your man-bun secrets?"

Jaime burst out laughing.

"What?" his mom said. "What did she say?"

Kate turned, smiled at their respective families gathered around, at the nosy and love-filled hallway, then turned back to Jaime and threw her arms around him. "I said, yes."

A cheer went up as she pulled back, turning away from him again, her gaze going to her father's. "And yes, for the long engagement."

Harry nodded approvingly.

But Jaime wasn't paying attention to any of them. He had Kate in his arms, albeit facing the wrong way.

Spinning her, he tugged off the moonstone ring then slipped the diamond on her finger and used the excuse of mistletoe overhead to kiss her senseless.

He kissed her as the doorbell rang, as voices echoed in the hall behind them, as bodies shuffled by them because they were blocking the path to the rest of the house.

He kissed her as her father cleared his throat, clearly telling him it had been long enough.

He kissed her until his head spun, until she pushed against his chest, and broke away for air.

But he still didn't let her go.

"I love you," she said, cupping his jaw.

"Hey, that's my line." He nuzzled her throat.

Behind her, the sounds of the party intensified, and Jaime knew their moment was almost over, but he still couldn't get his hands to release her. Though, realistically, he wasn't trying very hard, not when it felt so damned good to have her close.

"You sure about this?" she asked as he helped her to her feet, and though she looked up at him with love, with trust, Jaime knew she still needed time and affection and patience and care, knew she'd give him the same back.

"More sure than I've been of anything in my life," he said.

Kate tucked herself into his side. "Good," she said. "Because you're stuck with me."

He laughed.

And then because he could, he kissed her again.

Being stuck with Kate wasn't a bad place to be at all.

EPILOGUE

PART ONE

Kate

"I DIDN'T GET a chance to give this to you," she told Jaime two days later, setting the small package she had tossed in the direction of the Christmas tree after that day at the mall on his chest.

They were naked in bed.

A common occurrence around the man.

Giggling to herself, she tugged up the blankets and nudged the package at him when he didn't immediately move to open the present. She'd forgotten about it in her excitement in showing him the lace. Then forgotten again in the rush to get to her parents' house and once more after the excitement of his family showing up.

The McLeod crew had hit the pause on presents, not wanting Jaime's family to be left out.

Then she'd had her time with her friends yesterday, and Jaime had spent Boxing Day with his family doing their own exchange and traditions . . . and she'd forgotten until she'd spied the palm-sized package on the carpet earlier. But his family had headed home earlier that day, her family was planning on a New Year's Eve present exchange, and she didn't want to wait to see his face when he opened it.

A little gift.

But one that was sure to make him smile.

"What's this?"

She rolled her eyes. "Open it."

He waggled his brows. "Is it a ring?"

Another roll of her eyes. A kiss pressed to lips she loved kissing. "Long engagement, remember?"

"Mmm," he said, winding his fingers into her hair and transforming her light kiss into one that had her heart pounding and moisture pooling between her thighs.

And circling back to naked. Mmm.

She pulled away when his fingers slid up, brushing his hand away. "Behave."

He nipped her bottom lip.

She nipped back. "Open it," she demanded. "Then you can get back to kissing me." A beat. "Everywhere.

The wrapping paper disappeared.

The box was open a minute later.

And then Jaime was laughing. That warm, slightly rough chuckle that slid down her spine and made her pussy clench. He glanced from the watchband printed with roosters up to her eyes. "We're going to have a Barry, aren't we?"

She grinned. "Yeah, we are."

A quick, hot kiss. "On that note," he said, pulling back and getting out of bed.

"Hey! Where are you—?" Her question cut off when he disappeared into the hall, and not that she minded seeing his sexy ass striding away from her, but he was naked, *she* was naked, and they were supposed to be getting back to sexy naked time.

Then he was back, a present in *his* hands.

He crossed over to her, plunked it in her lap. "Open it, Red."

Since Kate loved presents, she didn't bother prevaricating. She tore open that paper, pulled the lid off the box, and . . .

Laughed until tears poured from her eyes.

It was a leash and harness. The same type as she'd seen Barry wearing in the picture Jaime had sent to her.

"Think you can teach him to carry our rings down the aisle?" he asked.

"I'm not sure roosters are trainable."

He tugged the box from her lap, dropped it to the floor. "My money's on you."

"No." Kate shook her head. "My money's on *us*."

Then while he was still smiling, she wrapped her arms around him and kissed the man she loved with everything she had.

She tasted that smile in her soul.

Yeah, her money was on them.

EPILOGUE

PART TWO

Heidi, Eighteen months later

SHE WAS WEARING a violet bridesmaid's dress and holding a leash.

Not the strangest sentence ever uttered.

Unless, perhaps she included what was on the other end of the leash.

Because she'd been escorted down the aisle by a rooster name Sir Fuzzy McFeatherston, or Fuzz for short.

He was cute. He was cocky—*ha*—and he was not happy to be on a leash.

Thankfully, though, the ceremony was wrapping up. The bride and groom—her best friend, Kate and her almost-husband, Jaime—were kissing. Soon she'd be able to put the rooster in the cage and she could get to drinking.

Because her best friend was getting married.

After an engagement she had promised Heidi would be extremely long, but had ended up sort of average because Kate hadn't been able to wait to make Jaime officially hers.

Barf.

She loved Kate, loved Jaime and how he treated her.

But she was losing her best friend.

So, yeah, maybe she was feeling a little mopey, but she wasn't going to let her funk ruin her friend's night. She was going to be the best rooster-wrangling bridesmaid there was.

Not maid of honor.

Kate hadn't wanted to hurt Kelsey or Cora's feelings, so they were all bridesmaids, all with different jobs.

But that was Kate.

The absolute best.

And now she was *married*.

God, they were growing up. Heidi sniffed and dashed away a tear as the officiant declared the newlyweds officially married before they strode down the aisle hand-in-hand.

And she strode—hand-in-leash?—with a rooster.

Well, if that wasn't an apt description of her dating life . . . she didn't know what was. She could find a man who wanted to sleep with her—*cough*, cock—but couldn't find one with staying power.

"Not the point," she muttered under her breath, somehow getting herself and Sir Fuzzy McFeatherston safely down the aisle, the rest of the bridal party pairing off and following her.

They snapped some pictures, but eventually the Fuzz got tired of the paparazzi and Heidi wrestled him into her arms and took him to the crate Kate had ready for him.

She was just bending to stick him inside, trying to slip off the harness without letting him escape when she felt someone come up behind her. Assuming it was Kate, she said, "I'm fine, Katie girl. Go enjoy your husband. I've got your"—she giggled, a twelve-year-old at heart—"cock well in hand."

Silence instead of her friend's cackling.

Shit.

Heat stained her cheeks, and Heidi yanked the leash and

harness out before slamming and locking the cage. Then she shored her spine and spun around.

Tall. Dark. A smirk on a gorgeous mouth.

One that grew as his gaze traced her down then up. "Sure you can handle that cock, baby?"

She *had* handled that cock.

Six months ago, Jaime's brother Brad had stopped in the Bay Area for a quick visit, and she'd had a few too many glasses of wine. He'd offered her a ride home . . . and then he'd given her a fucking *ride*.

So yeah, she'd had that cock, and, she couldn't lie, it had been *incredible*.

But . . . he'd been gone before she'd woken the next morning.

And she might be tough on the outside, she might be a strong, independent woman who hadn't been expecting a ring and a relationship, but she'd thought she at least warranted a note or a text or a fucking goodbye.

Heidi sniffed. "I've handled plenty of cocks in my life," she said, chin lifting, eyes narrowing. "And none are more than I can handle."

She pushed past him.

He snagged her arm.

She yanked it free, stepped back when he went to grab her again. "Don't," she snapped. "Just because I made a mistake once doesn't mean I'm easy prey now."

A cocky—no pun intended—smile. "Mistake? I happened to think we were—"

"*That* was you're mistake," she said, glaring. "*Thinking*."

Pretty hazel eyes flared. "Baby—"

"Not your baby."

A sigh. "Heidi."

"Yes, Brad, groomsman, who should be paying attention to

his brother's wedding instead of bothering a woman who *isn't interested?*" It wasn't a sweet question, for as sickly saccharine as her tone was.

"I think—"

She rolled her eyes. "Not *that* again."

Heidi didn't mean to, but it all happened so fast.

Brad grabbed her arm.

She shoved him back at the same time the crate door burst open and Sir Fuzzy McFeatherston shot out of the pen.

The rooster took off running.

Brad lost his footing, crashed into a waiter, who was carrying a large tray of appetizers.

The food went flying.

Brad went flying . . . into the cake table.

Sir Fuzzy McFeatherston went flying, feathers scattering in all directions.

The tray came down.

And Heidi didn't think she'd ever forget the sound of it colliding with Brad's head.

Nor how much joy it gave her.

At least until she turned back for the bridal party, promptly tripped over the fucking rooster . . . and ended up sprawled across Brad's chest.

Fuck, she loved that chest.

—Bad Bridesmaid Coming March 1st, 2021

BAD BRIDESMAID

Heidi's story is coming March 1st, 2021!
Preorder your copy www.books2read.com/badbridesmaid

BILLIONAIRE'S CLUB

Bad Night Stand

Bad Breakup

Bad Husband

Bad Hookup

Bad Divorce

Bad Fiancé

Bad Boyfriend

Bad Blind Date

Bad Wedding

Bad Engagement

Bad Bridesmaid

ALSO BY ELISE FABER

Billionaire's Club (all stand alone)

Bad Night Stand

Bad Breakup

Bad Husband

Bad Hookup

Bad Divorce

Bad Fiancé

Bad Boyfriend

Bad Blind Date

Bad Wedding

Bad Engagement

Bad Bridesmaid (March 1st, 2021)

Gold Hockey (all stand alone)

Blocked

Backhand

Boarding

Benched

Breakaway

Breakout

Checked

Coasting

Centered

Charging (December 28th, 2020)

Caged (March 2021)

Love, Action, Camera (all stand alone)

Dotted Line

Action Shot

Close-Up

End Scene

Meet Cute (April 5th, 2021)

Love After Midnight (all stand alone)

Rum And Notes

Virgin Daiquiri

On The Rocks

Sex On The Seats (April 26th, 2021)

Life Sucks Series (all stand alone)

Train Wreck

Hot Mess

Dumpster Fire (February 15th, 2021)

Roosevelt Ranch Series (all stand alone, series complete)

Disaster at Roosevelt Ranch

Heartbreak at Roosevelt Ranch

Collision at Roosevelt Ranch

Regret at Roosevelt Ranch

Desire at Roosevelt Ranch

Phoenix Series (**read in order**)

Phoenix Rising

Dark Phoenix

Phoenix Freed

Phoenix: LexTal Chronicles (**rereleasing soon, stand alone, Phoenix world**)

From Ashes

To Smoke (January 25th, 2021)

In Flames

KTS Series

Fire and Ice (Hurt Anthology, stand alone)

Riding The Edge (December 7th, 2020)

Stand Alones

Someday, Maybe (YA)

ABOUT THE AUTHOR

USA Today bestselling author, Elise Faber, loves chocolate, Star Wars, Harry Potter, and hockey (the order depending on the day and how well her team -- the Sharks! -- are playing). She and her husband also play as much hockey as they can squeeze into their schedules, so much so that their typical date night is spent on the ice. Elise changes her hair color more often than some people change their socks, loves sparkly things, and is the mom to two exuberant boys. She lives in Northern California. Connect with her in her Facebook group, the Fabinators or find more information about her books at www.elisefaber.com.

facebook.com/elisefaberauthor

amazon.com/author/elisefaber

bookbub.com/profile/elise-faber

instagram.com/elisefaber

goodreads.com/elisefaber

pinterest.com/elisefaberwrite